JENNIFER S. ALDERSON

Death by Puffin

A Bachelorette Party Murder in Reykjavik

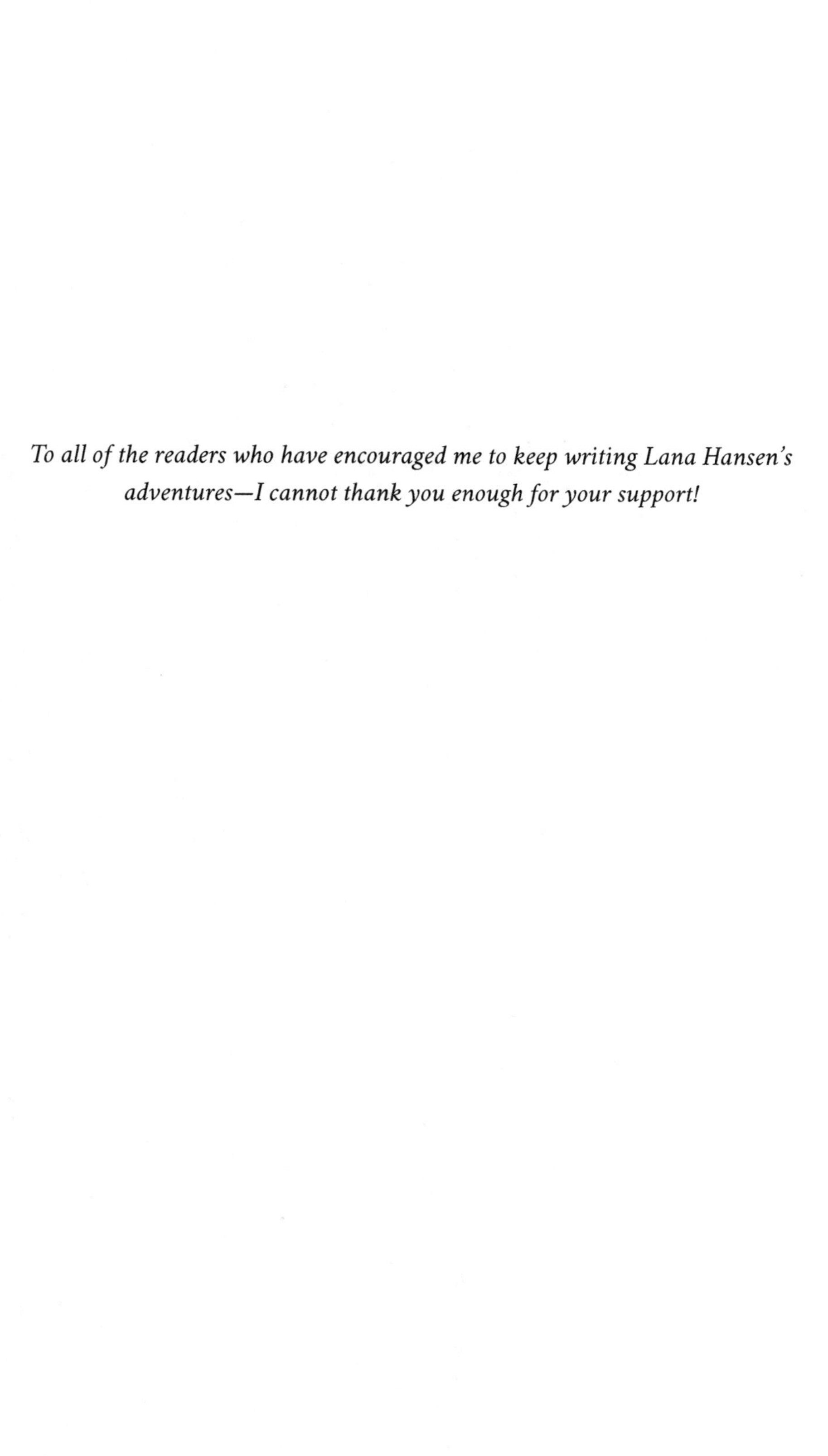

To all of the readers who have encouraged me to keep writing Lana Hansen's adventures—I cannot thank you enough for your support!

Contents

1

Storm Brewing

Sunday—Reykjavik, Iceland

Lana Hansen stared outside, taking in the storm brewing over Faxaflói Bay. Gale-force winds whipped rain and hail across her hotel's windows, temporarily blurring her view of Mount Esja, rising high above Reykjavik's skyline.

Despite the breathtakingly beautiful sight before her, Lana couldn't enjoy it. Right now, it felt as if the turbulent weather mirrored the storm raging in her heart and mind. Her job and relationship were both on the fritz, and after a week of soul-searching, she still couldn't see a way out of either predicament.

I really need to talk to Willow, Lana moaned internally, knowing it was not possible. Willow Jeffries was Lana's best friend and one of the most sensible people she had ever met. Whenever Lana had a problem, Willow managed to cut right to the heart of the matter and often offered her a perspective she had not yet considered. Yet as much as Lana wanted to call her, it was the middle of the night in Seattle; she couldn't risk waking up Willow's baby girl, Zoe. Knowing her best friend was effectively unavailable sank her into a deeper depression, so much so that she barely registered the knock on her hotel room door.

Only when the knocks increased in intensity and frequency did Lana snap out of her daze and rise to answer the door.

Did I order room service and forget about it? she wondered as a troubling thought struck. *Am I having temporary lapses in consciousness now, on top of everything else?*

"Lana Hansen, I know you are in there. Open up," her visitor insisted.

The person's voice caused her to sprint to the door and yank it open. When she saw the petite African American woman standing in her doorway, she blurted out, "What are you doing here?"

The woman's hands flew to her hips. "Is that any way to greet your best friend?"

"No, it most certainly is not." Lana pulled Willow in for a hug, careful not to tug on the plethora of tiny braids cascading down her back. "I seriously thought I was hallucinating. I was just wishing I could call you, and now you're standing in my doorway. I can't believe that you are here!"

"Me, either," Willow laughed. "Are you going to invite me into your room?"

"Of course, come on in." Lana stepped aside. To her delight, Willow had a large suitcase with her. "Gosh, how long are you planning on staying?"

Instead of answering, Willow let her bag fall to the floor as her hand flew to her nose. "What is that smell?"

She laid a hand on Lana's arm. "What happened here—were you robbed and they trashed the place? Or are you having a breakdown?"

Lana looked around the space with a critical eye. Dirty cups were stacked on top of the minibar, and used towels hung off of the backs of the chairs and furniture. But the *pièce de résistance* was Lana's bed. The sheets and pillows were twisted up into a tower-like mass and covered with a scattering of crumbs and candy bar wrappers.

"Tracey Emin could turn your bed into a work of art," Willow said, no hint of a joke in her voice.

Lana grimaced. She only knew about the contemporary artist's installations—her most famous featuring her own unkempt bed—because of Willow. Her best friend loved to visit Seattle's many museums and galleries far more than she did.

Still, Lana couldn't get past her friend's sudden arrival. "Seriously—what are you doing here? You have a beautiful baby girl at home who needs your care and attention far more than I do."

"And a wonderful partner who was willing and able to take a few days off work to care for her." Willow took Lana's hands and smiled. "Besides, Dotty promised to help out."

"I don't know how good she is with kids," Lana grumbled.

"Look, I am certain Zoe will be well-cared for, so stop worrying about her for me. You sounded so depressed the last few times we talked, I was really worried about you. And after Dotty caught me up to speed, even more so. I have seven whole days to spend with my bestie to try to help her—that means you—get out of this crazy slump. At least, if you don't mind a roommate."

Lana threw her arms around Willow as she choked back her tears. "Thank you so much for coming over. I really need a friend right now. I feel so lost, I just don't know what to do anymore."

"I figured as much, which is why I knew a long video chat wouldn't be enough to sort this out." She rubbed Lana's back and let her cry it out for a moment, before gently pulling out of their embrace.

"However, I cannot sleep in a room this dirty. We are going to have to let the hotel cleaners back inside, but we should probably tidy up a little bit first, so they don't throw you out."

Willow gazed around, apparently taking in the sorry state of Lana's room, before asking, "I know you told Dotty you needed time to get your head sorted, but this is not what I expected. Have you been holed up here since you arrived?"

"Pretty much. I didn't come here to see the sights."

Willow's deep sigh sent a wave of irritation over Lana. "What did you think I was doing—hiking a glacier or soaking in a hot spring? Alex broke my heart, and my boss thinks I'm a magnet for murderers. I haven't been having the best month. Can't I just lie here and wallow in self-pity for a few more days?"

When Willow's frown deepened, Lana plopped back down onto the couch and pulled a blanket over her head. *Maybe if I stay under here, she will leave me be.*

Willow's laugh was not friendly as she tore the blanket off. "Frankly, I hoped that was exactly what you were doing. You are in Iceland—I figured this was therapy by nature. Come on, it's time to rectify this situation."

Willow held out her hand.

Lana pushed further back into the couch's fluffy cushions and reflected on her friend's statement. "How are we going to do that?"

"I've booked us in at the Blue Lagoon. Our bus leaves in an hour."

Lana shook her head. "I'm not ready to mingle with tourists. Can't we use the hotel spa, instead?"

"No, we need to get you out of this room and back into the world. That might be the only way for you to get over this wallowing depression, because this…" Willow glanced again around the dirty space. "…is not normal. Besides, I bet if you allow your mind to focus on other things, it will be easier for you to see your problems from a distance. And if we are lucky, we can figure out the solution to both of them, together."

"You aren't going to take no for an answer, are you?"

Willow shook her head.

"Then I have no choice but to go with you. Let me find my coat."

Willow grimaced as she sniffed in her friend's direction. "Even though we are going to a pool, I still think you should shower first and change into something clean. You don't smell fresh."

Lana looked down at her stained and crumpled clothes. When had she changed last? Or showered?

Willow pulled open the chest of drawers. "It's empty. Where are your clothes?"

Lana pointed to her suitcase, open on the floor next to her bed.

"You haven't even unpacked yet?" her friend cried. "You truly are a mess."

She pulled a T-shirt and jeans out of the suitcase, then tossed them to Lana as she walked towards the bathroom. "These look relatively clean."

Lana snatched them out of the air and pulled the T-shirt up to her nose, using it to cover her reddening cheeks. "Thanks. I'll be back in a minute."

2

Relaxing in the Blue Lagoon

"You are so right, Willow. Coming here was an excellent idea," Lana said as she reveled in the warm water of the steamy pool. Soaking in the Blue Lagoon with her best friend by her side, Lana could feel the tensions of the past few weeks finally melting away.

Children splashed each other as their parents bobbed in the warm waters, many with a mud mask already applied. A thick layer of steam hovered over the surface of the blue water, the pools surrounded by dramatic rock formations created by cooling lava millions of years ago.

Despite the vastness of the complex, it was quite busy, especially around the swim-up bar. Lana and Willow had spent the first hour splashing each other like kids as they explored the complex, taking in the waterfall and hot tubs, as well as the in-water massages and mud masks on offer.

After the pair enjoyed a fruity cocktail, Willow pointed to a distant area of the complex. "What do you say we find a quiet spot and have a chat?"

"Sure, okay." Lana's enjoyment faded slightly at the thought of having to confront her woes again, but that was why Willow had flown all the way from Seattle, she realized. Seeing the sights was secondary. "Good idea. I'll follow you."

As they slowly swam towards a smaller pool that seemed to be less busy, Lana took in the strange juxtaposition of the Blue Lagoon's location. From one angle, the steamy pools appeared to be an oasis in the middle of a rugged and desolate landscape. This was definitely the shot she had seen on social media. However, when Lana turned the other way, the industrial-looking entrance building and hotel lining the pools dominated her view.

Lana chose to focus her eyes on the Instagram-worthy views and ignore the buildings behind them. Thanks to the thick layer of steam that flowed out of large vents and across the water's surface, she could barely see Willow paddling around somewhere in front of her. Being outside in the cold air and yet being toasty warm thanks to the hot water was surreal and slightly magical. Even though it was June, the temperatures hovered around fifty degrees.

Once they had entered a quieter area of the Blue Lagoon, Willow twisted her long braids into a bun, then laid back against the side and kicked out her legs, allowing her body to float. "This is heavenly."

Lana mimicked her friend's position, feeling the heaviness of the mineral-rich water.

"Have you ever seen such a vibrant color of blue?" Willow asked.

Lana shook her head. "Never. It's beautiful, but a little stinky. I guess that's the sulfur."

"True, though it's not as pungent as some of the sulfur hot springs I've visited in the Pacific Northwest," Willow replied. "So, now that you've had a chance to relax a little, it's time to talk. Which do you want to tackle first—Alex or your job?"

Lana felt her stomach clench, glad that the steam hid her irritated expression from Willow. "It doesn't really matter; both are pretty painful subjects. My boss wants to ground me, and my boyfriend has been lying to me for months. Take your pick."

"Why don't we start with your job. I have some interesting facts to share with you about the death rate on your tours."

Lana resisted the urge to plunge her head under the water and stay there.

"I did some online research, and it is shocking how many tourists die every year while on vacation."

Lana's right eyebrow shot up. "What do you mean?"

"Admittedly, adventure sports are the biggest causes, but there are plenty of stories about tourists who tripped while hiking and fell down a cliff, kayakers who tipped over and drowned, and swimmers who overestimated their skills and got pulled out to sea—you name it, someone has died doing it."

"We don't hike many cliffs or do much kayaking during our city tours," Lana quipped.

"Even so, there are plenty of more mundane cases of tourists walking in front of a bus while reading a map, or diving into a hotel pool and breaking their necks. I even read that drunk tourists regularly fall into the canals of Amsterdam and drown."

Lana opened her mouth to interject, but Willow pushed through. "And it seems to be a popular thought that killing your spouse abroad is easier to get away with than doing it at home. I found several cases of spouses poisoning, drowning, and even running over their better halves with rented cars, while on vacation."

A chill ran up Lana's spine as she thought back on the many ways her clients had killed their loved ones during a trip she was leading. One had even tried poisoning her, as well, but Lana was lucky enough to have received immediate medical treatment.

"It's a good thing the cops can't see your online search history," she joked, trying to change the subject.

"True, they would probably lock me up. But I figured you wouldn't really listen to me if I only searched online, so I went straight to the source."

Lana felt her forehead crinkle. "What do you mean?"

"I talked to your boss. Dotty and I had a real heart-to-heart on this one. She was convinced that you had become some sort of murder magnet. But after we chatted and she looked up a few figures for me, we discovered that Margie is the true angel of death at Wanderlust Tours."

Lana shot up, creating a rippling wave that raced over the pool as she stared at Willow. "What on earth are you talking about?"

She thought on her fellow guide, a spunky sixty-year-old who had been leading tours since Wanderlust began. "Margie is one of the nicest people I have ever met. There's not a bad bone in her body."

"Sweetie, there are none in yours, either. Did you know that thirty-two people have died during her tours? If anyone should be grounded, it should be her."

Lana rolled her eyes. "It wasn't her fault one of their tour buses got caught in that avalanche. That has to account for ten, maybe fifteen of the casualties. It was a miracle that she wasn't on it. And there were no murderers in her group—only an unexpected snowstorm and a few clients with bad hearts. Besides, she's been leading groups for fifteen years. I should hope her fatality rate would be higher than mine."

"Okay," Willow said brightly, "but I also had Dotty look up how many of your tours were casualty free, and it was far more than she thought. Did you know that you have led forty-seven tours, but only eight of them involved a death?"

"Nine—if you count Venice."

"Neither the victim nor murderer was on your tour!"

"But I still got sucked into the investigation—and in a big way," Lana wailed.

"Hey, you two might want to keep your voices down. Your conversation sounds pretty private and the way the water reflects sound, we can hear everything you are saying."

Through the mist, Lana could make out a young blonde in a string bikini calling out to them from across the pool. She was surrounded by three other young women sporting the same bottle-blonde hair and heavy makeup. From this distance, the four could almost have been sisters. A fifth woman with darker hair paddled around in front of them.

"Can't they just mind their own business?" Willow mumbled.

"Sure, okay," Lana replied loudly as she waved to the group, before leaning in closer to her friend and whispering, "Those five are staying in the room next to ours, and I would rather not get into a fight with them. They make a lot of noise as it is, and I would hate for them to increase the volume as a way of getting back at us. And they do have a point—this is a private conversation about me possibly being a murder magnet. I'd rather that it not get around."

"I don't know, they might give you a wide berth if they knew," Willow laughed before wagging her finger at Lana. "I don't mind waiting to continue our chat until we are back in your room—but you are not getting out of this."

"Fair enough. Besides, maybe it's better if we wait. How often does one get to experience the Blue Lagoon, and with their best friend, no less? I say we book us an in-pool massage. They look heavenly."

"Sounds great. Follow me!" Willow splashed Lana before quickly swimming away from her friend, cackling as she did.

Lana laughed heartily for the first time in days, before chasing after her.

3

Partying Too Hard

On the bus ride back to Reykjavik, Willow and Lana had trouble staying awake. Thanks to the mineral-rich waters of the Blue Lagoon and the heavenly massages they'd treated themselves to, both were extremely relaxed and rested. For the first time since she had arrived, Lana felt as if there might be a solution to her problems, after all. Though she wasn't there yet, with Willow's help she hoped to resolve both crises before the week was over. After all, she couldn't hide out in Iceland forever.

After they got back to the hotel room, Lana flipped the television on to a music channel, and the two friends flopped onto the freshly made bed. Both women's eyes fluttered shut, and soon Lana heard Willow softly snoring.

Lana picked up a magazine and soon felt herself drifting off. She woke with a start an hour later. When she noticed that it was fast approaching seven in the evening, Lana gently shook her friend's shoulder. "Time to wake up."

Willow's eyes shot open, then blinked slowly as she took in her surroundings. "That felt good." She pushed herself and stretched out her arms. "I haven't slept that deeply, well, since I had Zoe."

"I'm so glad. I haven't felt this relaxed since I got here. Thanks again for dragging me to the Blue Lagoon."

Willow squeezed her arm. "Anytime."

"Say, it's already seven—"

"Wait, what? How can that be? It's still light outside."

They both looked to the hotel room windows, the heavy curtains still open, and took in the bright skies. "I know, it takes a little getting used to. But Iceland is so far north that the sun doesn't set until almost midnight this time of year."

"Geez, we must be around the same latitude as Alaska!"

Lana giggled at her friend's shocked reaction. "I guess we are. Are you hungry? I could use a bite to eat. Should we order room service or explore the city a bit before we have dinner?"

"Now that the room's been given a good scrub, I would rather dine in, if you don't mind. I have no desire to get dressed up right now. But before we order, can we talk about Alex?"

"It's been such a lovely afternoon—can we please save the heavy stuff until tomorrow?" Lana begged.

Willow frowned until she noted Lana's pleading expression. "Alright, so long as you promise to talk to me tomorrow. I'm only here a few days, and I want to help you get through this crisis. No offense to this beautiful country but I would rather not have to keep coming to Iceland to see you—it's cold here!"

Lana chuckled. "It's a deal. But tonight, I would just love to chat about silly things over a glass of wine."

"I'll toast to that." Willow grinned as she sprung up and crossed over to the minibar. After examining the broad selection, she picked up a mini-bottle of Merlot and cracked it open. "We should order some appetizers to go with our wine."

She looked down at the room service menu before pouring them each a glass. "They have a cheese platter with Icelandic fruits and rye bread. How does that sound?"

"Perfect," Lana murmured as she took her wine from Willow's outstretched hand. "I could get used to this life."

"Me, too." They clinked glasses in midair and took a sip.

"Yum, that's smooth," Willow declared before turning down the music and walking over to the hotel's telephone to order. As soon as the volume decreased, a thumping bass became audible.

"Gosh, these rooms are really not soundproof, are they? I hope we weren't playing our music too loud for our neighbors."

"I don't think that's the problem," Lana replied. When a high-pitched giggle rose up, she muttered, "I think our neighbors are getting ready to party again."

Willow shrugged. "No skin off my nose. Now, where was I? Oh, yeah, room service." She smiled over at Lana. "That sounds so fancy every time you say it."

After ordering, Willow said, "They warned me it might take longer than normal because they have a lot of orders to get through. I hope you are not too hungry."

Lana waved her concern away. "I'm not in a rush. That sandwich at the Blue Lagoon was pretty filling."

"And scrumptious. I've never had salmon prepared quite like that. I'm glad we tried it. Now, let's just hope we both stay awake until the food arrives."

A scream of laughter pierced the walls, followed by dance music being turned way up.

"What the heck?" Willow exclaimed.

"It's the bachelorette party. They have been getting louder and louder every night they've been here. Before they arrived, it was a peaceful hotel room," Lana said miserably, disappointed by the rowdiness of the guests next door. "I understand that they are excited about the upcoming wedding and want to send their friend off right, but they don't seem to take into account that there are other guests on this floor."

"You warned me that they had been making a lot of noise, but this is ridiculous!" Willow practically shouted to be heard over the music next door.

"I can't say that I disagree. If we're lucky, they'll go out dancing soon and we can get to sleep before they return."

When the shrieks of laughter intensified further, Willow stood up and strode to the door. "Enough is enough. I am going to ask them to keep it down."

"Don't waste your breath—they are the most self-absorbed group of young people I've met in quite a while. And based on their clothes and conversations, they seem to have rich parents paying their bills. They either aren't aware that they are being so loud or don't care. If we complain, I am afraid they will only get rowdier, to spite us."

"Maybe the hotel can move us to a quieter room?"

"I already asked. They are full, but did promise to let me know if something frees up."

"Do you know when the wedding is taking place?"

"From what I have overheard, this Friday. They appear to be making a week of it."

"Wow, they must be rich—Iceland isn't cheap."

"Considering almost everything has to be flown or shipped in, I guess the high prices are justifiable."

When something hard bonked against the wall between the two rooms, followed by another shriek of laughter, Willow fumed, "This is unacceptable. If you don't want me to talk to them directly, then I'm going to call the front desk."

Lana threw up her hands. "Be my guest."

Willow's grievances were heard by a front-desk employee who assured her that he would take care of this situation straight away.

"If it makes you feel better, he said two other rooms had already called to complain," Willow said as she put down the receiver.

A few minutes later, a loud knock on the neighboring door made both women grow silent, curious to see how the group of partying women would react to the hotel employee's request.

A fit of laughter was their response. "Are we surrounded by old biddies?" one of the women shrieked into the hallway. Lana blushed in response, wondering whether she was indeed overreacting. Here they were, trying to enjoy a week with their friend before she got married. Were they not entitled to have a good time? Their joy and happiness was a painful reminder of what she and Alex had once had, Lana realized, which might be why she was reacting so negatively to their frivolity.

Stop thinking in past tense—technically, we are still a couple, she scolded herself.

For how much longer was her choice.

"I hate to say this, but if the other guests continue to complain about the noise, then I will have to ask you to leave the hotel," the employee said in a loud voice, certainly for the other guests' benefits.

"No you won't," one of the women retorted. "Audrey could buy this hotel and fire you if she wanted to. Whoever called to complain should get a life and let us lead ours. If the others don't like hearing us have fun, they can move. There are plenty of other hotels in Reykjavik."

"Maybe we should change hotels," Lana suggested. "It doesn't sound like they care about the other guests or are planning on taking it easy this week."

"Tabitha! Stop being so rude. I apologize for any irritation we may have caused," another female voice said.

"Audrey, it's your party, and you are entitled to have fun—"

"But not at other people's expense. Elaine was right earlier, we haven't been respectful of the others," Audrey said. "I apologize for upsetting your other guests. We are only staying here one more night before we leave for a tour of the island. We will do our best to keep it down."

"Thank you," the employee said, the relief audible in his voice.

After their door closed, the noise level dropped considerably. The young women continued to party and chat, but the music and voice volumes were much lower.

"That's better. At least we can talk normally now," Willow said. "I just hope they aren't going to be on the same trip we are, or it's going to be a really long week."

"That would be extremely annoying." Lana said before Willow's words sank in. She whipped her head around to face her friend. "Wait—what do you mean, the same trip?"

"I was going to surprise you at breakfast. Dotty has booked us on a three-day tour of the southern part of the island. We leave the day after tomorrow."

"No way! I am not going on an organized tour. I came here to get away from them!"

"No—you came here to sort out your relationship and career, and that's not happening in this hotel room. All you are doing is wallowing in self-pity, which is obviously not helping. Besides, why did you pick Iceland if you didn't want to explore the great outdoors? That is what it's famous for."

"I picked Reykjavik because it was the next flight leaving the airport." Lana stood up and paced the floor. "What if someone gets killed during our trip? That would only prove that I'm a sort of magnet for killers. At least I can't hurt anyone here in the hotel room."

Willow's exasperated sigh made clear that she was done with this conversation. "We are in one of the world's most beautiful places. If hanging out in this glorious nature for a few days isn't enough to heal your soul, then I don't know what will."

When Lana began to shake her head, she added, "And if you don't go, then you have to call Dotty and tell her why we skipped the tour."

Simply thinking about how that conversation would go was enough motivation to change Lana's mind. "Alright, you win—we'll go. But I can't promise you that I'm going to enjoy it."

4

Love and Trust

Lana took another bite of the skyr, letting the thick yogurt-like substance roll over her tongue. "This is such a funky taste. I like it, but it's a totally different sensation that the yogurt we have back home."

Just as her eyes fluttered closed so as to savor the flavor more intensely, Willow set her coffee cup down on the table with a hard bang.

"Alright, it is officially tomorrow, and you have had some breakfast." She nodded towards the spoon in Lana's hand.

"Can't I finish my yogurt first?" She had hoped to enjoy her meal in peace, before Willow forced her to examine her life choices. Yet based on her friend's stern expression, she wouldn't be able to delay this conversation much longer.

Willow shook her head.

Lana pursed her lips but nodded in assent.

"So, let's make certain I have all of the relevant facts before we dive into the Alex conundrum. You are angry with your boyfriend for lying to you about his participation in radical protest actions carried out by the Earth Warriors—yes?" Willow paused until Lana nodded. "At least he wasn't cheating on you."

"He lied about what he was doing with his life—not just once, but three times. And so convincingly, too. That's what hurts the most."

After she had discovered during her tour in Venice that Alex had repeatedly

16

lied to her about participating in several Earth Warriors protests, Lana's initial reaction had been to break up with him. Lies had torn her first marriage apart, and she had no desire to repeat history. However, she couldn't just throw away what they had built up. So instead of staying in Venice and hashing it out with him, she had fled the city.

"Say what you will about Alex, but the Earth Warriors are incredible. Their publicity stunts attract the media's attention to worldwide problems like no other organization can, and their actions have helped to initiate real change. Instead of being angry with him, you could be proud that he was taking part."

Willow must have noticed that Lana's eyes were about to bulge out of her head, because she quickly added, "Even though I have huge respect for what the organization does, I do not approve of Alex lying to you about his involvement. He should have told you the truth—there is no doubt about that."

Her friend's heartfelt sincerity brought tears to Lana's eyes. More than anything, she needed someone to understand her anger and frustration. She grabbed Willow's hands and squeezed tight. "Thank you."

Willow locked eyes with her. "Alex lied to you, but was it with malicious intent? I don't think so. He got too wrapped up in the protests and probably couldn't figure out how to tell you without upsetting you. If he hadn't been arrested for that murder, he may never have told you."

"Which is what freaks me out. I had no idea he was taking part in those daredevil actions. If I didn't see that coming, what else could I be missing? Ron had been cheating on me with his assistant for months, and I hadn't noticed."

"Oh, Lana, you can't compare Alex to your ex-husband. Ron makes a living out of being a manipulative liar. What else could you expect from such a weasel?"

"That is putting it rather harshly. Not all magicians are manipulative."

"Yes, they are—that is what makes them good at what they do," Willow insisted. "Besides, Alex has assured me that he is done with the Earth Warriors."

Lana stared at her friend. "Wait a second—Alex called you? Is he trying to win you over so you will pressure me to take him back?"

"No, that's not it. But he does know we are best friends, and he is truly concerned about you. Reaching out to me was his only chance at getting in contact with you. He loves you, Lana, and feels stupid for lying to you for so long."

"He told me that, too," she whispered, thinking back to their last conversation in Venice.

"What I don't quite understand is: why are you so angry with him? Is it because he lied, or did he do something else that you haven't told me about? Taking off on your own is a pretty drastic step. You are usually more level-headed than that; I'd have expected you to stay and talk it out."

"I suppose I should have, but I was wound up so tight I was worried I would say something that I would later regret. Three murders on three consecutive tours was messing with my head. Dotty threatening to put me on temporary leave didn't help matters, and Alex's lies on top of everything else was too much to bear." She bowed her head, a tear forming at the corner of her eye. A few months ago, everything had been going so well with her job and relationship. She still couldn't fathom how horribly wrong it had all gone in such a short span of time.

Willow wrapped her hand over Lana's and squeezed. "I totally understand. When Jane and I were trying to decide whether to have a child or not, we had a lot of disagreements about the timing and method. A few of our discussions got pretty heated, and I ended up staying at my parents' for a few days, just so we could both cool off. If I hadn't done that, I might have walked away from her." Willow's voice wavered as she also wiped a tear from her eye. "What a waste that would have been. Now we have a beautiful daughter, and I can't imagine being with anyone else. Jane really is the perfect partner for me."

Lana pulled back and stared at her friend. "I had no idea!"

"Only our parents knew what we were going through. The decision to adopt or undergo IVF treatments was too personal to open it up to a general discussion. But we aren't here to discuss my past, but your future."

Willow gazed out into space as if she was trying to order her thoughts before continuing. "I am relieved to hear it's just the lies and nothing else that sparked all this trouble. After Alex lied to you the first time, he probably felt as if he had no choice but to keep doing so."

Lana crinkled her forehead. "What do you mean?"

"Think about it—after he told you he'd only participated in one protest, there was no way back for him. If had changed his story the second or third time you asked and admitted to taking part in several, you would have felt betrayed and been upset with him. It was definitely a stupid move on his part, but somewhat understandable."

Lana considered Willow's words. "You do have a point. If he hadn't been arrested, the television news would not have replayed all of his reckless actions during those other protests. And if they had not done that, I probably never would have known how extensive his involvement was. If only he had trusted me enough to tell me the truth from the start, we wouldn't be in this mess."

"Maybe he was afraid you would try to talk him out of participating. The stunts they pull are pretty dangerous."

"I suppose you're right. If it had been a one-time thing, I would have understood. But Alex had been keeping his involvement in those protests a secret for months! Willow, put yourself in my shoes—how would you feel if Jane had done the same thing?"

Willow closed her mouth and thought a moment. "Pretty irritated and angry," she admitted, "But I love her enough to find a way to push past it and not let it tear us apart. Alex didn't cheat on you or do anything to compromise your relationship. You cannot forget that."

"But his actions do make me question my unrestricted faith in him to tell me the whole truth, and not just the bits he wants to share."

"Give yourself a little more time before you decide what to do. But if you think you want to save your relationship, you may want to get in touch with him."

"I know I should, but I'm certain he'll want an answer, one way or the other."

"True. Maybe you could send him a text message, just to let him know you haven't written him off completely."

"Sure, what's the emoji for 'I love you but am not certain I can trust you'?"

"Hmmm, not sure off the top of my head," Willow laughed. "What would he have to do to get back on your good side?"

Lana ticked on her fingers. "Stop with the protests, and preferably stop working with the Earth Warriors altogether. But he's an adult so I can't forbid him to remain a member, and I would feel like a heel for even asking him to give it up."

"Okay. Anything else?"

"Figure out how to enjoy life more so he doesn't need to seek adventure through such an extreme outlet. Maybe he can take up a hobby or learn something new."

Willow nodded. "That sounds reasonable. And if he does what you ask, you'll take him back without condition? Can you trust him to not lie to you again?"

"Trust him at his word?" Lana bit her lip. "That remains the million-dollar question. His lies have brought back all sorts of nasty memories, like how Ron used to message to say he was practicing late, when really he was with his assistant. Thanks to our jobs, Alex and I communicate primarily by telephone, and I don't want to be constantly wondering if he's telling me the truth about what he's really doing."

"You can't live like that," Willow agreed.

"No, I can't," Lana sighed. "So I have to figure out how to let it go, or break up with him."

Willow squeezed her arm. "Give yourself a little more time. But don't give up on your relationship just yet."

Lana frowned at her bowl of breakfast. "Could we please mark the Alex part of this conversation as 'to be continued?'" she asked before picking up her spoon and shoving a large serving of skyr into her mouth.

"Sure. I'm here for six more days. But I do have one more question for you before we go back into vacation mode."

Lana's eyebrow shot up.

"Why didn't you tell me about the last three deaths? Dotty told me how they took place on back-to-back tours. That sounds really traumatic. I wish you had called me."

"You have a baby daughter, a business, and so many more responsibilities to deal with. I couldn't burden you with my troubles, as well, and especially not over the phone. Dotty started calling me an angel of death, Willow. These past few weeks haven't exactly been the high point in my budding career as a tour guide."

"Lana, I'm not just Zoe's mom, I'm still your friend. I have room in my life for both of you. Please call me anytime—day or night."

When Lana began to shake her head, Willow added, "It's not just for you, it's for me, as well. Since I've had Zoe, my life consists of feedings, cuddling, and computer work when she's napping. It's almost impossible to meet up with friends because her sleep schedule is so erratic—especially now that she's teething. Listening to your adventures keeps me in the loop of life. So I will always have a shoulder for you to cry on. Though I'll warn you right now, it'll probably be stained with milk and baby food."

When Lana began to tear up again, Willow looked down at her plate, filled with an array of tiny sandwiches made of brie, cod, and salmon. "Everything looks so delicious. Where to begin?"

Before she could pick one up, a loud shriek made them jump.

5

Breakfast of Champions

Monday—Reykjavik, Iceland

Both Willow and Lana turned towards the urgent cry. Sitting behind them was the bachelorette party, all dressed in matching pink sweat suits and bunny slippers. The only one with a tiara on appeared to be woozy and—as Lana watched—her head tipped forward and her face landed in her plate full of pastries.

"Someone help!" one of her friends cried. The only dark-haired member of their party pulled the unconscious woman's head up by her hair, getting her face out of her breakfast.

As if on autopilot, Lana sprung out of her chair and raced over to the girl. Responding immediately to ill or endangered clients was part of her tour guide training, and she couldn't ignore a cry of distress, even if the person was annoying.

By the time she got the table, the tiara-wearing woman had regained consciousness and was attempting to right herself.

"Nothing to see here," the dark-haired woman exclaimed when Lana approached.

Lana ignored her and knelt down to study the woman's face, noting that her eyes were glassy and her cheeks devoid of color. "This young lady needs to be examined by a doctor."

When she reached out to take the woman's pulse, the raven-haired girl slapped her hand away. "We don't need a doctor to tell us what's wrong. Audrey is diabetic and has been having a lot of trouble with her insulin this week."

"Why isn't she wearing a medical bracelet?" Lana demanded.

"Ugly," the sickly woman mumbled.

"That may be so, but it might save your life one day," Lana chastised before rushing over to the breakfast bar and pouring a glass of orange juice. She raced back and held it out to the diabetic. "Drink this, it should help even out your sugar levels."

The dark-haired girl took the drink out of Lana's grasp and held it up to the sick woman's lips. She drank most of the juice in one gulp, then leaned back in her chair and closed her eyes, letting the liquid do its work.

"Much better," she muttered, though her eyelids remained shut.

"I'll have to remember that trick for the next time."

"I hope there won't be one. Diabetes is nothing to mess around with."

Both Lana and the dark-haired woman studied their tiara-wearing patient until her cheeks began to flush again and her eyelids fluttered open. When she half grinned at her friend, the dark-haired woman squeezed her hand before turning to Lana.

"Thanks for helping Audrey out. I'm Elaine, and this is Bianca, Destiny, and Tabitha. We're the bridesmaids." Elaine waved towards the other women sitting at the table.

The three had long blonde hair cut in a similar fashion and fake nails painted with the same glittery polish. Their catwalk-ready makeup would have taken Lana hours to apply. Destiny was a little shorter and less busty than the rest, whereas Bianca was taller and more voluptuous than the others.

It appeared that the three were copying the haircut, manicure, and makeup of their tiara-wearing friend. Yet even with bits of pastry stuck to her face, it was obvious that Audrey spent more money on her appearance than the rest. Even her pink sweat suit seemed tailored to fit her waspishly-thin waist and generous bustline.

"Speak for yourself—I'm the maid of honor," Bianca snapped.

"Of course, how could I forget. It's not like you haven't reminded us of it constantly or anything," Elaine replied, her eyes rolling.

"Happy to help," Lana said just before Bianca stood up and got in Elaine's face.

"You know, I am sick of your snotty attitude, Elaine. I don't know why Audrey invited you to the wedding, let alone made you a bridesmaid. You're an employee, not a friend—"

"Hey, that's not nice. Yes, technically Elaine works for our family, but she's been a good friend to me for many years. I would not have wanted to get married without her standing by my side." Audrey wrapped an arm around Elaine's waist and squeezed.

Lana was surprised to see that Elaine seemed to be more embarrassed than uplifted by Audrey's heartfelt words.

Audrey looked up at Lana, a smile on her face. "Thanks for the OJ. It really does help. My blood sugar levels aren't usually as topsy turvy as they have been this week. I attribute it to the jet lag."

"The stress of the trip and your upcoming marriage aren't helping," Elaine added.

Audrey jutted her chin up in the air. "It's a small price to pay to become Gunnar Jónsson's wife. I'll be fine."

"Congratulations on your upcoming nuptials," Lana exclaimed.

Audrey smiled broadly. "Thanks. It seems so unreal, getting married to Gunnar here in his native Iceland. It really is a dream come true."

"That's why you are getting married here, of all places," Willow exclaimed, then blushed when Audrey looked up at her quizzically.

In her rush to lend assistance, Lana hadn't noticed that her bestie was standing right behind her.

"Sorry, that sounded weird," Willow stammered as pink dots formed in her cheeks. "It's just, Iceland's not really known as a romantic destination and foreigners usually aren't allowed to marry in another country, at least not without filling out a ton of paperwork."

The bride-to-be's expression softened as she began to chuckle, and Lana also noted that color had returned to Audrey's face. *The orange juice really has helped.*

"We don't have to go through all of that because Gunnar was born here. I had always wanted to get married abroad, but figured it would be on a warm, tropical island, not one covered in volcanoes and ice."

Willow and Lana laughed, causing the bridesmaids to join in.

"Audrey's not so bad," Lana leaned in and whispered to her friend, who nodded in agreement.

"You sound American to me. If he's from here, how did you and Gunnar meet?" Willow asked.

Audrey smiled. "Gunnar was born in Reykjavik, but his family moved to California when he was young. He's as American as they come." She paused before adding with pride, "His parents own John's Sporting Goods stores."

"Oh yeah, I know that name," Willow replied.

"I didn't realize the owners were Icelanders," Lana added. John's Sporting Goods was the largest and best-known chain of sporting and outdoor equipment in the United States; she had assumed the company was American-owned.

"Me neither, until I met Gunnar. His dad opened the first store here in Reykjavik before he imported the concept to California twenty years ago. From there, they expanded quite quickly across the nation."

"Are you all from the Golden State?" Willow asked.

"No, we're from Oregon."

Bianca held up a finger to interrupt Audrey. "I'm a transplant from San Francisco. My family is still in the Bay Area, but I like Portland so much I think it's going to be my home for many years to come."

"That's nice, Bianca, but I was in the middle of a story." Audrey smirked at her friend. "So, like I was saying, a few months ago, Gunnar moved up to Portland to manage the new stores his company just opened in the area. We met at a party, and once we spotted each other across that dance floor, it was as if he only had eyes for me," Audrey said wistfully as she clasped her hands to her chin.

When Lana smiled down at Audrey, Tabitha leaned in between them and glared up at her. "Hey, how did you know the orange juice would help?"

When Destiny and Bianca mimicked Tabitha's expression, Lana automatically took a step back. It seemed that the three blonde bridesmaids didn't want her to get too chummy with the bride-to-be.

"It looked like she was having a hypoglycemic reaction. I learned that orange juice trick as part of an extensive EHBO course that I took before becoming a tour guide. The glycerin in the juice is absorbed quickly into the blood and helps counteract the insulin overdose," Lana explained.

"You're a tour guide? That's perfect. We were just trying to figure out where we should go dancing tonight. We heard the clubbing scene here is spectacular. We only have one more night in town before we have to explore the great outdoors, and I want to make the most of it."

It was clear from Bianca's sarcastic tone that she was not looking forward to their planned trip. Lana wasn't the only one to notice the displeasure in her voice.

"What's the matter—are you afraid your Jimmy Choos won't survive the hikes?" Destiny cackled.

"We don't have to worry about ruining our shoes," Audrey broke in. "Gunnar is sending over all the gear we will need, sometime today."

"Oh, that makes life easier. But why didn't you say something before we left? Half of my suitcase is filled with hiking gear that I bought especially for this trip," Tabitha groused.

Audrey waved her friend's concern away. "It was a surprise to me, too, but really sweet of him, don't you think? If you can't return the clothes and gear after we get back to Seattle, let me know and I'll pay for it."

Tabitha beamed at Audrey as she patted her shoulder. "Thanks, you really are a good friend."

"As long as her wallet stays open…" Destiny whispered to Bianca.

"But I was so looking forward to shopping with you here. You did promise…" Tabitha's bottom lip was already jutting out in a pout.

"We can still go," Audrey said brightly. "Maybe after breakfast?"

"You can shop anytime!" Bianca cried. "I thought we were going to ride the wild horses together. There's a day tour that leaves in a few hours that sounds perfect."

The bride-to-be's brow crinkled. "That's true, I did promise we would—"

"But I booked a facial for me and Audrey at the hotel's spa! We've been talking about doing that since we got here," Destiny said.

Audrey threw her hands up in the air. "Ladies—there is only one of me!"

Lana watched their conversation with dismay. It seemed as if the three blondes had different relationships with Audrey and were trying to pull her in diverse directions. Considering her fragile health, she hoped that the bridesmaids would give the bride-to-be a break.

Willow leaned over and whispered, "Can we please leave? I would like to see some of Reykjavik today."

"Sounds great to me."

They began retreating towards the exit, almost afraid to turn their backs on the increasingly heated conversation, when Bianca's snobby tone stopped them in their tracks.

"So, tour guide, where should we go clubbing?"

It took all of her self-control not to snap at the young woman. "First off, my name is Lana, and this is my friend, Willow. Secondly, I have no idea where you should go because I have never been to Iceland before. Why don't you ask the hotel's receptionist?"

"But isn't it your job to know those kind of things?"

Lana began to bite down on her tongue but changed her mind, fed up with the girl's arrogance. "When I am actually leading a tour somewhere, yes. If you don't want to ask the hotel staff, then you'll have to buy a travel guide or search online. Right now, I am on vacation, just like you all."

When Audrey began to giggle, Bianca's eyes narrowed at Lana. "Hey, thanks for helping Audrey, but we've got it from here. Right, girls?" She turned to the others, and the pair of blondes nodded emphatically and crossed their arms over their torsos, as well.

Only Elaine did not; instead she rolled her eyes at the group and stuck her hand out to Lana. "Thanks again. We'll see you around."

Before she and Willow could turn to leave, Destiny's squeal pierced their ears. "Mimosa time, ladies!"

The five picked up their flutes of champagne and orange juice off the table and held them up high. "To the future Mrs. Jónsson!"

Audrey giggled as she sipped her drink, blushing at the attention.

Lana couldn't help but stick her nose in again. "Are you sure you should be drinking alcohol right now?"

Audrey only laughed. "How often does a person get married? It's my party, I'll drink if I want to. Right, girls?"

She held up her glass to another round of cheers. "I'm so glad you all could make it over. It feels strange not having any family here, but you are all my best friends, and that's close enough."

After they had downed their drinks, Audrey looked to Willow and Lana. "Gosh, would you two like a mimosa? You were so kind to help me just now. It's the least I can do."

"That's alright, we were just about to head out."

Audrey sprung up and hugged Lana tight. "Thanks again for helping me out."

6

An Unexpected Visitor

Lana squirmed in the young woman's uncomfortably long embrace. When Willow ticked a finger on her watch, Lana pulled back from the bride-to-be.

"You're welcome. You look much better now. I hope you get to enjoy the rest of your day."

When they turned to leave, their passage was blocked by a strikingly attractive man and a luggage trolley, both rapidly approaching Audrey's table.

"Pookie—there you are!" The man's deep voice rose over the crowd. With his imposing height, broad shoulders, shaggy blonde hair, and rugged jawline, Lana could easily see him gracing the cover of a fashion magazine. Next to him stood a hotel porter holding onto the luggage trolley filled with bags from John's Sporting Goods, as if his life depended on it.

"Gunnar! I'm so glad to see you." Audrey jumped out of her chair and held her arms wide.

Her fiancé rushed towards her, but before they could embrace, Bianca sprung in between them. "Aren't you two taking a weeklong break from each other, to make your honeymoon even more romantic?"

Gunnar glared at her and took Audrey's hands, pulling her forward so that Bianca had to move back.

"I couldn't stand being away from my beautiful bride for another minute."

"To be—you aren't married yet," Tabitha reminded them, moving in so close to Gunnar that they were practically touching.

Destiny did the same as she laid a hand on his arm and smiled up at him seductively. "You really shouldn't be here, you know. It's bad luck."

"No it's not. Seeing me in my wedding dress before I walk down the aisle is," Audrey said as she shoved her friends aside and wrapped her arms around Gunnar's neck.

"Are the bridesmaids actually hitting on him?" Willow whispered.

"Could be," Lana murmured in response, studying the odd scene before her. The three blondes' actions reminded her more of the evil stepsisters in *Cinderella*, jealous that their younger sister had found love while they remained spinsters.

"What are you doing here?" Audrey asked.

"I wanted to personally deliver your tickets to you." Gunnar kissed her cheek before gently untangling her arms from around his neck, then pulling a pile of tickets out of his coat pocket. "Not all of the tour operators have gone paperless yet, unfortunately. You'll need these tomorrow."

When the hotel porter standing behind him coughed discreetly, Gunnar added, "As well as these." He patted the trolley. "Here are all of the clothes you will need on your trip. Audrey gave me your measurements." He turned to the porter and handed him a fifty-euro note before the young man scurried back to the front desk.

"I chose your outfits myself, pookie. You'll have to take pictures of my darling fiancée, girls. She's going to look hot!"

"Did you choose our clothes, as well?" Bianca leaned over the table as she lowered her sweatsuit's zipper, ensuring he could see her ample bosom, if he so chose.

He did not. Instead, he grabbed his fiancée's hand before responding, "I sure did. Lucky for you, Bianca, we sell clothing for every body type."

Lana's jaw dropped. *Is he body-shaming her?* How dare he imply that Bianca was fat! Sure, she was taller and rounder than petite little Audrey, but by no means overweight.

"Excellent, I'll be thinking of you, then, every time I get dressed," Bianca continued in a sultry voice, apparently unaware of his implied insult.

When Audrey turned sharply and glared at her friend, Bianca reddened. "That came out wrong. Thanks for the clothes, is all I meant."

"Are you looking forward to seeing some of Iceland's most impressive natural phenomenon?" Gunnar turned to the rest and rewarded them with a smile so pure, it would make angels sing. "I am envious of you—the Skaftafell Glacier and Gullfoss Waterfall are two of my favorite places in all of Iceland."

While Elaine seemed to be impervious to his pearly white teeth, the other three bridesmaids swooned under his grin and gaze.

What is wrong with these people? Lana wondered. Maybe Willow was right. Gunnar was an attractive man, but these were supposed to be his future bride's best friends. Luckily, Audrey seemed pretty oblivious to her friends' behavior.

"We can't wait to see all that Iceland has to offer. It's just too bad you can't join us," Tabitha purred.

"But then it wouldn't be a bachelorette party if I tagged along, would it?" he laughed easily.

Gunnar turned back to Audrey and lowered his voice. "Is the paperwork we discussed in order?" Unfortunately for him, the deep timber of his voice made his words resonate around the table.

Audrey nodded and smiled up at him like a puppy expecting a treat. "Yes, everything is taken care of—just as we discussed, my love."

"And your aunt doesn't know?"

The bride-to-be giggled. "No, that witch does not have a clue. If she did, I bet you money she would fly over and try to prevent us from getting married. Not that she could stop the wedding, but it would be so embarrassing to have her charging around saying we shouldn't be together."

"Yeah, we don't need that extra stress in our lives," Gunnar agreed.

Lana wondered whether he knew what the word "stress" meant—he seemed so carefree. In some ways, he and Audrey appeared to be a perfect match.

She knew that she and Willow should walk away, but listening to their conversation was akin to watching a soap opera that she couldn't tear her eyes away from.

Gunnar rested his forehead against Audrey's. "Good thing she doesn't know, then. I cannot wait until Friday." He tilted his head down to kiss her, when his eye caught her plate, filled with French pastries.

"Babe—you aren't seriously going to eat all of that, are you? Don't forget that you have to fit into that Vera Wang on Friday."

"I know, but everything looks so delicious. I couldn't resist trying a few." Audrey's tone had gone all whiny.

"They're just empty calories that you don't need right now." He shook his head as he picked a chocolate croissant off of Audrey's plate and took a bite, before critically studying his fiancée's face.

"You are looking a little bit puffier than normal. Why don't you stick to yogurt and fruit until the wedding? Skyr is what keeps Icelanders so healthy and virile. All of my relatives are going to be there, and I don't want them to think you're a fat cow."

"Why, that little—" Willow growled.

Lana could only shake her head, at her friend and the situation. Nothing good would come of them butting into the conversation, and Lana doubted Gunnar would care what she or Willow thought.

Audrey blushed. "You're right. You're always looking out for me. You'd better take this out of my sight before I eat it all."

"That's a good girl." Gunnar rewarded her with a kiss on the nose before he grabbed her plate and proceeded to gobble up everything on it.

"Get Audrey a bowl of skyr, Destiny," Gunnar commanded between bites. Lana was shocked by the casualness of his tone, and even more so when Destiny sprung up and did as he asked.

"Are you kidding me?" Willow turned away from them and pretended to gag. "Can we leave now?"

Lana grabbed her wrist and squeezed. "Let's get out of here." She cleared her throat. "Say, it looks like you are feeling better and are in good hands," she said loudly, with a nod to Gunnar. "Take care today, alright?" She waved at the bride-to-be before turning to leave. As she did, she could almost feel the daggers shooting out of the three blondes' eyes.

"See you around," Willow added as they walked away.

Lana heard Gunnar ask, "Who are those two?"

"Just a couple of tourists."

Before they reached the exit, one of the blondes whisper-shouted to her friends, "I hope we don't run into them again. Did you see what they are wearing? Those two are fashion disasters. I would be embarrassed to walk out the door with that on."

"Oh, honey, you would never buy something so atrocious in the first place. But don't worry your pretty little head, Tabitha. We're leaving tomorrow for that tour, and I seriously doubt they are going to be on it. Audrey said it was one of the most expensive and exclusive tours available on the island—isn't that right, Gunnar?"

Willow's feet faltered, and Lana knew what her friend was thinking. Willow may be small in stature, but she was no pushover. Before she could turn around and give them a piece of her mind, Lana wrapped an arm through hers and propelled them forward. "They aren't worth it, Willow. And we still have to sleep next door to them for one more night."

When they were out of earshot, Willow erupted. "What a horrid group! You take care of their friend, and they repay you by belittling us? Have you ever met such a spoiled group before?"

Lana chuckled. "Yes, almost every time I lead a tour. Money makes some people think they can boss others around. It's quite depressing, but a fact. And from the looks of the clothes and jewelry they have been wearing these past few days, those girls have a lot to spend. They must make a killing at what they are doing, or their parents are providing them with generous allowances."

"I would guess the latter—not a single one of them looks to be a day over twenty-five, and I doubt they work for a living. And did you see their nails? With fakes that long, you sure can't type! And that Gunnar is a real piece of work. Why would anyone want to marry him? I almost hope for Audrey that the wedding doesn't happen," Willow growled, luckily softly.

He might have been a controlling jerk, but Gunnar was also gigantic and Lana did not want to get into any sort of altercation with him. "I don't know what Audrey sees in him, either. But she's not the only one who is interested in him, from the looks of things."

"I know what you mean. All three of the blondes seem to swoon whenever he looks their way. They aren't even trying to hide their flirting." Willow glanced back before adding, "What a strange situation. Does Audrey not notice? Or is it a turn-on—that she gets to marry the guy everyone wants to have?"

As they approached the door, both turned to regard the couple. Gunnar was standing behind Audrey and massaging her shoulders as he winked at Tabitha. To Lana's dismay, Tabitha smiled back, instead of looking away in shock.

"It's hard to say. From the looks of it, it could go either way," Lana replied. "Gunnar is rich, or at least his family is. Did you notice his vintage Rolex? Maybe Audrey is willing to turn a blind eye as long as he gives her full access to his credit cards and bank accounts."

Willow nodded. "Could be. Though I do recall one of them making a comment last night about how Audrey could buy this hotel. Though that might have been a lie to get the hotel employee to back down."

Lana regarded them critically. "If she is richer than him, maybe she is looking for a trophy husband. Gunnar would certainly fit the bill."

"You have a good point. For some people, social standing is more important than true love."

After they entered the lobby, Lana stopped and locked eyes with her friend. "Can we put those spoiled brats out of our minds and focus on enjoying Reykjavik? The bus tour leaves early in the morning, and I would like to see some of the city before we go."

"That sounds great. Let's just hope that their tour leaves at a different time than ours tomorrow. With a little luck, we won't run into them again."

7

On The Road Again

Tuesday—Day One of the Southern Island Tour of Iceland

"Are you ready for an adventure?" Willow asked, a smile splitting her face. She and Lana had just settled into two comfy seats on the touring bus that would whisk them around the southern tip of Iceland for the coming three days.

"I will be, once the coffee kicks in." Lana stretched her arms out over the empty chair in front of her and hid a yawn in her bicep. When she drew her hand back, her fingertips glided over the soft leather.

"Dang, Dotty went all out—as usual." She took in the leather seats and video screens built into the back of each chair. A menu listed the selection of beverages and snacks available during their journey, several of which were alcoholic concoctions Lana had never heard of. The tour was clearly intended for the high-end crowd, as the luxuriousness of their transportation attested.

Willow ran her hand over the red velvet armrest separating their roomy seats. "She told me it was the tour she books her guests into."

They were about to embark on an adventure-filled three days exploring the waterfalls, volcanoes, geysers, and glaciers that gave Iceland its nickname, the Land of Fire and Ice. On their last day, they would even get to visit an island full of puffins and search for whales.

"It looks amazing," Lana said with a nod to the screen displaying a slideshow of photographs of the natural wonders they would be visiting.

The enticing photos showed off the dramatic rock formations, high valley walls, surreally empty landscapes, and powerful waterfalls. The videos of wild horses galloping across green fields, whales breaching, and puffins staring into the camera with their large orange beaks and curious-seeming black eyes brought a smile to Lana's face.

"You know, I'm actually looking forward to this." She couldn't wait to be a tourist for a change. And having her best friend by her side made the trip even more special.

"Well, good. You might just enjoy yourself, after all," Willow teased.

They were set to depart in five minutes, but the bus built to seat thirty was suspiciously empty. Lana wondered whether it was the high price tag that kept tourists away or the extremely early departure time. So far, it was them and three more couples, all seated towards the front of the bus. She and Willow had headed straight to the back, where they could stretch out and hopefully sleep a little before they reached their first destination—Skaftafell Glacier.

"Thanks for forcing me to join you on this trip," Lana half joked.

"We should both thank Dotty for booking us onto this tour. It looks like we are in for quite a treat," Willow said. "A five-a.m. departure time is pretty early, but I'm glad that means we will have more time to explore the Skaftafell Glacier before it gets too crowded with other groups."

"True. It's good they are taking the popularity of the sites into account. And it is pretty wonderful knowing we can both just kick back and let someone else deal with any complaints or delays. Heck, I could fall asleep and no one would try to get me fired!"

"Ah, the freedom to do what you want for a change. But it must be strange to be an off-duty guide on a tour. I do hope our guide is up to snuff. Speaking of which, have you thought any more about what we talked about…"

Lana felt her stomach clench, knowing Willow was referring to her job. Yet, her attempt to get Lana to talk about her future at Wanderlust Tours was interrupted by a squeal of laughter.

"Oh, no," Lana whispered and sank down into her chair at the sight of the bachelorette party hovering around the front of their bus.

"What is it?" Willow began to rise but Lana pulled her back down.

"Audrey and her friends are outside the door."

Willow's nose crinkled. "Oh, no. They aren't really joining this tour, are they?"

"I think this is the bus. It's the right tour company, in any case," Tabitha exclaimed in her high-pitched voice.

Bianca rapped her knuckles onto the bus's door. "Hey, are you the three-day tour of the Southern Island?"

"Isn't the sign on the dashboard big enough for them to read? It fills half of the windshield, for goodness' sake!" Willow muttered as their tour guide, a sprightly woman in her thirties, rose and opened the door, before bending down to talk to the ladies. A few moments later, she descended the stairs and loaded their many suitcases into the space under the bus.

"Should we see if there is a later departure?" Lana offered, knowing that her friend was on the edge of saying something nasty to the bachelorettes. The irritation in Willow's voice was as clear a signal as an air alarm.

Before she could respond, the three blonde bachelorettes boarded the bus and collapsed into seats in the middle, speaking so loudly that everyone could easily hear them. They were all wearing bunny ears on their heads and a fake-flower necklace in a rainbow of colors over their brand-new outdoor gear.

"Oh, man, that club was fire," Destiny muttered.

"It's too bad we had to get up so early, otherwise we could have stayed longer," Tabitha added, her voice just as sleepy.

Elaine, the dark-haired bachelorette, trailed in behind them. She didn't have her bunny ears on, but was wearing the same rainbow-colored necklace and hiking gear replete with the John's Sporting Goods logo.

"Audrey couldn't have," Tabitha sniggered. "The bouncer had to carry her to the taxi after she passed out in the bathroom."

Lana's eyes widened in shock; she knew a diabetic shouldn't be so casual with her alcohol consumption because the results could be deadly.

"I don't get it. She'd been ordering virgin cocktails most of the night and then bam—out like a light. Some bachelorette party," Bianca groused.

"What do they call that when people pretend to be ill so often so that they actually become sick—Munich syndrome? Or was it Manchester syndrome?" Tabitha said.

"Munchausen's syndrome," Elaine said with a frown. "But I don't think she's faking it…"

"Oh, my head!" Audrey groaned as she climbed onto the bus, holding onto the railing with one hand and her head with the other. She still wore her tiara, as well as the same fake-flower necklace that the others had on. "I don't know why my medications are so out of whack on this trip—I feel like I've drunk an entire bottle of vodka."

"How would you know what that feels like?" Tabitha snapped.

"It was a figure of speech," Audrey snarled. "Can we cut out the drama today? I'm still pretty groggy from last night."

Tabitha's eyes narrowed, then suddenly flew open as a smile curled her lips. "You're right. My head is still throbbing, too. I'm sorry for taking it out on you."

Audrey shrugged. "It's okay, but we still have four more days to get through before the wedding. Maybe I shouldn't drink any more alcohol for the rest of the trip. What do you say, should we cut out the booze?"

"Speak for yourself," Destiny laughed.

"Thanks for the tip, mom, but no," Tabitha replied.

Audrey rolled her eyes at her friends and walked past them, flopping down in the seat directly in front of Willow and Lana. As she did, the bride-to-be glanced back at the pair, her eyes widening in recognition.

"Hey, it's the tour guide and her friend."

Lana noticed Willow's knuckles tensing up as she gripped the velvety armrest. "Hello, again. We didn't expect to see you today."

Tabitha and Bianca rose and glanced back at Lana and Willow.

"We can say the same about you." The two blondes scrunched down in their chairs and began whispering loudly.

Elaine moved to sit across from Audrey, irritating Willow further.

"I hope we don't have to walk too far today. I feel completely wiped out." Elaine confessed to Audrey.

Willow leaned in close. "I am going to see if there are seats available on another tour. I would rather not have to listen to them moan all day long, if we can avoid it."

"You can ask, but I'm not going to hold my breath. This bus isn't even half full. I doubt they have another tour departing today."

As discreetly as she could, Willow approached their guide and leaned in to make her request. Based on the woman's head shakes, Lana had to assume that there were no other options. Willow's flight back left in five days—avoiding the bachelorette party was not worth missing her flight home or this trip.

"No joy," Willow confirmed upon her return. "The next tour leaves in three days—that's too late for me. The guide said we are about to depart, so what do you want to do? We can bail on our little adventure, or just ignore them."

"I say we ignore them. The tour does look spectacular, and it would be a shame to miss seeing it more of Iceland, simply because of them."

"That's the spirit! Let me just tell her we are staying." Willow sprung up and spoke briefly to the guide, who nodded, then leaned over to talk to the driver. Before Willow was back in her seat, their bus was pulling into traffic.

"Excellent. We've got a five-hour ride ahead of us. I say, it's time for a little shut-eye."

8

An Island Wedding

Lana managed to get ten glorious minutes of rest before Audrey's shrill voice woke her.

"Could you keep your voices down? My head is killing me!" the bride-to-be screeched at her friends. "I wish I'd brought aspirin."

"I have some," Elaine said. She dug around in her large handbag until she pulled out a packet of aspirin, a jar of pills, and a water bottle. "Geez, it's good you asked because I forgot to take my own pills. Here's an Advil for you."

After her friend passed her the pill, Audrey nodded towards the jar. "What are you taking?"

"Penicillin. It's really bitter," Elaine said and smirked. "The water helps get rid of the taste."

"That's pretty heavy-duty medication. What's wrong with you?"

Elaine grimaced. "Legionnaire's disease—can you believe it? It is one of the many hazards of being a gardener, I've learned."

"But how is that possible?" Willow gasped.

Willow was a fanatic gardener, so Lana figured she was concerned for her own safety—otherwise she would have stayed out of their conversation.

"Moldy potting soil. At least, that's what I believe to be the culprit, and my doctor agrees. She said contact with potting soil accounts for half of all the reported cases. I had developed a horrible cough that only got worse. It's rare enough that it took weeks before my doctor diagnosed it correctly."

"How interesting," Tabitha said in a bored voice before plopping down next to Elaine and hip-bumped her into scooting over. "Hey, tour guide…"

"My name is Lana," she growled, "and this is my friend, Willow."

"Okay. What can you tell us about the weather? Do we really have to wear those heavy parkas Gunnar gave us? They are not at all attractive; I don't know why he said they were. We all look like marshmallows."

How should I know, was on the tip of her tongue. Instead, she answered politely, "According to our hotel's receptionist, it is going to be in the low forties and rainy all week."

"Great, that's almost freezing. Why couldn't you have married a Hawaiian, Audrey?" Tabitha grumbled.

"Trust me, I would have rather gotten married on a palm-fringed beach. The photos would have been far more Instagram-worthy. But it's what Gunnar wants. And this way, all of his family can join us."

"You would think he's rich enough that he could fly them all over to San Francisco," Tabitha muttered.

Audrey ticked her tongue against her teeth. "Money's not the issue—his grandparents are really old and refuse to fly anywhere. He doesn't want to get married without them."

"At least we can see the Northern Lights while we are here. That's what Iceland is so famous for, right?" Bianca said.

"I don't know if it is only visible in the winter or all year round," Destiny said while looking at Lana. "Tour guide, I mean, Willow, do you know if we can see the Northern Lights from our hotel tonight?"

The women's self-absorbed attitudes had pushed Lana's patience to the limit. "How many times do I have to say it—my name is Lana, Willow is my traveling companion, and we are not your tour guides! I do not know if we can see the Northern Lights, though I doubt it. I, too, believe it is only visible in the winter months. I know nothing about the country and cannot help you. Coming to Iceland was a spur-of-the-moment decision, and I didn't take time to read up on it on the plane ride over. If you are so keen to learn more, talk to our guide or buy a book."

Willow hid a smile behind her hand and averted her eyes to the window.

"Why would I want to lug a book around when I can just search for the answer online?"

"Then why are you bothering me with your questions?" Lana huffed.

Tabitha held up her phone. "The cell reception out here is horrible."

"Of all the rude—" Lana cut herself off, not wanting to escalate this exchange into a confrontation. "Look, it's really early. If you don't mind, I would like to sleep a little before we arrive at our destination. Could you move back to where you were sitting and leave Willow and me be?" She turned on her side, facing the window, and closed her eyes.

As the bridesmaids rose, Lana heard one of them whisper loudly to the others, "What's with that guide, anyway? She sure seems cranky. I'm glad she's not leading this tour."

Lana rolled over to face Willow and whispered to her friend, "Those women are driving me crazy. When we get to our first stop, can we please do everything humanly possible to avoid them?"

"Happy to oblige," Willow whispered back.

9

Breaking the Rules

"Alright, it's time to wake up, folks." Their chipper tour guide was up in the front of the bus holding a microphone. The speaker to which it was attached was cranked up so loud that it could wake the dead. Lana pulled her head off of Willow's shoulder and groggily took in her surroundings, confused until she recalled they were in a bus on their way to an Icelandic glacier.

After the turbulent start to the journey, Lana and Willow were finally able to fall into deep slumber. Other than a brief lunch stop at a gorgeous black sand beach, Lana and Willow had slept most of the long ride, figuring they would need all of their energy for the glacier walk.

"In a few minutes, we will be entering the Vatnajökull National Park where we will get to walk across the famous Skaftafell Glacier."

Pictures of the two spots she'd mentioned flashed onto the little screens. The names of the park and glacier were so full of consonants, Lana wasn't certain she could pronounce either. She half listened to their guide's enticing descriptions as she stretched and twisted her body, trying to wake up. When she looked to Willow, her friend's yawn caused Lana to do the same.

Soon their vehicle was pulling into a massive parking lot built for buses. A young woman and man dressed in matching parkas emblazoned with the Ice Masters logo waved the bus into a parking spot and then climbed aboard. They were both blond and looked to be in their early twenties, though it was hard to tell for certain. Their thick pants, gloves, and parkas disguised most

43

of their features.

"Welcome to Skaftafell Nature Reserve in the Vatnajökull National Park!" the female guide exclaimed. "I am Helga, and this is Petur. We will be your guides today during your glacier walk. You are in luck; it is overcast but dry, which means you'll be able to see the entire Kverkfjöll mountain range."

Like the best duos, the male guide continued seamlessly where she left off. "In a moment, Jeeps will take us further into the park. We do have a moderate hike ahead of us, so you may want to stretch your legs before we continue. It is a twenty-minute ride to the trailhead and start of our glacier walk."

After giving them a minute to stretch, the pair ushered the thirteen guests into three of the awaiting Jeeps. On the ride to the trailhead, the Kverkfjöll mountains were their constant companions. They rose high above the flat landscape, their tips still covered in white despite it being June. The vast fields dotted with tiny shrubs seemed to go on forever. It was starkly beautiful, but Lana would not want to get lost while hiking out here.

The Jeeps unloaded their passengers by a raised wooden platform set up in the middle of the tundra-like field. Lana and the rest of the group gathered around their guides and waited for their instructions.

"Have you ever seen such a magnificently desolate place before?" Lana asked in a soft voice. Being in the presence of such beauty always made her feel reverent. She was used to hiking through old-growth forests and mountain ranges, but had never seen anything like this before. There was something so primal and raw about this place.

The rest of their group, however, was not as impressed.

Destiny crossed her arms over her torso as her bottom lip jutted out. "I thought this was a forest."

"No, this is the glacier part. Ice, remember? We're going to walk over part of one. At least, that was what the brochure said," Elaine explained.

"Don't glaciers melt in the summer?" Tabitha added.

"Not the big ones, like they have here. But I saw on their website that the ice cave already melted."

"They shouldn't have put that into the brochure if it melts. That's false advertising, isn't it?"

"Who are you going to sue—Mother Nature?"

In an attempt to put distance between herself and the idiotic ramblings of the bachelorette party, Lana shuffled closer to their guides, and Willow followed suit.

"Okay, folks, we have a fifteen-minute walk to the ice field. Before we go, let's fit everyone with a harness and helmet. We will save the crampons and axes for the ice," Helga said.

Petur held up a bag of equipment. "Let's start with the harnesses." He passed a harness, a series of adjustable straps that went around a person's waist and thighs, to each of his clients.

Bianca held hers far away from her and pinched her nose closed, staring at it as if it was a used jockstrap. "We don't have to wear these ugly things, do we?" she asked Audrey.

"We're already dressed like marshmallows. I doubt we'd feel anything if we fell down," Tabitha added.

Audrey turned to their guides. "Why do we need to wear these? We are going on a hike, not climbing a mountain. Am I right, girls?"

Lana rolled her eyes at Willow. Her friend leaned in. "Seriously? They refuse to wear their safety gear because it's not sexy?"

"With a little luck, you won't actually need the harness, helmet, or ax, but they are all required if you want to join the tour. The harnesses are so we can quickly rope up if the path becomes too slippery."

She then held up a small metal ax with thin, yet sharp-looking blades. "The ice ax is so you can arrest your fall if you slip and slide down the glacier's face. Trust me, even those thick snowpants won't protect you from the sharp rocks and crystalized ice. And if you fall and hit your bare head on the compacted ice the wrong way, you're as good as dead, which is why we wear helmets," Helga explained in a neutral tone.

"I guess we don't have a choice," Audrey said before stepping into her harness and tightening the straps.

Next came the helmets, their canary-yellow color making it easy for a rescue crew to spot them, should something horrible happen, according to their guides.

Once they were all fitted with their gear, the two guides took up the lead and the rest followed.

The first fifteen minutes was a pleasant walk through rolling hills, with the taller mountains in the background. As she led them to the ice, Helga explained how glaciers were formed. Lana was surprised to learn that they are made from fallen snow, not frozen water. The snow was slowly compressed into ice by the weight of the new snow accumulating on top of it, according to their guide.

"After it's squeezed long enough, most of the air is forced out—that's why glacial ice appears to be blue," their guide explained.

Her further descriptions of the ice caves and tunnels that were prevalent in the winter months sounded incredible. If it wasn't so darn cold in the dead of winter, Lana would be tempted to come back to see them. She had never been a fan of the extreme cold, and the current temperatures were already pushing her limits of comfort.

Apparently she was not the only one. Minutes later, Willow shivered as she pulled her jacket tighter around her neck before turning back to look at Lana. "It is really pretty here, but couldn't you have picked a warmer place to hide out in?"

Lana chuckled. "I was thinking the same thing. It's even colder than the Pacific Northwest."

Soon they were at the base of the glacier. To Lana, it looked like a gigantic frozen river flowing off the mountain's flanks, had frozen in place.

Both Lana and Willow stopped when they reached the edge of the ice. Neither woman had stood at the base of a glacier before. The massiveness of it unnerved her; locked inside that glistening spectacle before her were millions of liters of unreleased water and power.

"You have to admit that this is a more inspiring view than the inside of your hotel room," Willow teased.

"You got that right." It was incredibly beautiful, but what surprised Lana most was the color and texture of the glacier. It was not a smooth, snowy white, as she expected it to be. Instead, chunks of dirt and stones were frozen into the upper layers of ice. Everything that blew onto its surface must freeze instantly and be trapped, she realized.

"Okay, folks, please gather around," Helga called out. "We are about to step onto the Skaftafell Glacier," the young female guide enthused as she made eye contact with everyone in the group.

"Before we set off, we need to go over a few rules. Most importantly—everyone needs to stay on the trail at all times! The ice changes as it shifts and melts, which is why we check these trails daily for your safety. The path is not that wide, so we will walk up the trail single file. It is a moderate hike, but the inclines can be quite slippery, especially since the sun is shining down on us today."

"After we all put these crampons on," her male counterpart said as he held up a contraption that reminded Lana of a bear trap, "we will set off. They are easy to attach to your boots. Give us a shout if you have trouble."

Both guides began handing out pairs of the metal contraptions that fit onto the bottom of their shoes. The steel frames were edged with sharp blades that cut through the upper layers of ice enough to provide them with grip as they climbed.

Lana was surprised at how easily they attached to their footwear, though she did wish she'd brought her waterproof boots, like the ones the bridesmaids were wearing, instead of her normal hiking boots. Gunnar really had set them up right.

Their guides first passed out their crampons before helping those who needed it. The bachelorette party was surprisingly quick with putting them on.

Lana leaned over to whisper to her friend, "If Petur was more attractive, would the bachelorettes have needed assistance?"

Willow suppressed a chuckle. "Undoubtably. Poor fellow, he's probably good-looking, but with all this outdoor gear on, we all look like the Michelin Man."

An older couple had trouble getting the crampons onto their boots so Petur graciously helped them. When both expressed anxiety at walking over the ice, he offered to stay by their side at the back of the group, so they didn't feel pressured to walk faster than they felt comfortable doing.

Once everyone had crampons on their feet, their guides handed out ice axes, warning everyone to be careful with the sharp blades.

Helga waved to catch their attention before addressing her group once more. "One last safety tip before we go. If the wind kicks the snow up, or we deem it too slippery, then we will stop and have everyone attach their harnesses to my rope. Which leads me to my next request—please heed any warnings we give you, especially if we ask you to stop!"

"Perhaps most importantly, have fun," Petur added. "Okay, let's head out!"

Helga took the lead, and true to his word, Petur stayed at the back to assist the older couple. The group set off, single file, ice ax in one hand and camera in the other. Lana and Willow gently pushed their way towards the front, glad to see that the bachelorette party was far behind them.

They had only been climbing for a few minutes when Helga suddenly raised a hand and yelled out. "Okay group, gather round."

She stood next to the edge of the trail and was busy wiping off the surface snow and dirt. When the bachelorette party was in her sightline, she said, "You were asking why we force you to wear all this safety gear. This is why."

Helga made a small circle with the blade of her ax, then used its blunt end to hammer against the newly made form. For a second the ice remained in place, before a sharp crack pierced their ears and the circle suddenly fell down, far into a fissure in the ice's surface. From where Lana was standing, the narrow opening seemed to grow increasingly blue the further down she looked.

"This is a crevice, which is essentially a fissure in the ice's surface. Some of these holes can reach hundreds of feet in depth, certainly deep enough to make rescue nearly impossible. Because it is summer, the ice is more susceptible to these crevices, which is why we check the trail every morning to ensure that none have formed under the route we want to take our groups on."

The group all leaned over a bit more to see better down into the deep hole.

"What makes crevices so scary is that you cannot always see them," their guide explained. "It is common for a thin layer of ice to form around the top, and once that gets dusted with snow, it looks just like the hardened path we lead you tourists up. Needless to say, leaving the trail could have lethal consequences—so don't do it!" She tittered away, again as if she was the funniest comedian in Iceland.

Willow leaned in and whispered in Lana's ear, "What is with that creepy laugh? Falling to your death doesn't seem funny to me."

"I don't know, but it does make me pay attention to what she's saying—more than our bachelorettes, by the looks of things."

"They do seemed to be more interested in their phones than our guides. Luckily, it's not your problem," Willow said, reminding Lana that this was not her tour to lead.

The first portion of the hike along the base of the glacier was easy going. Once they started to climb up, however, the crampons came into play. Though it was reassuring to know that they kept her feet from sliding back down the icy face, it was slow going pulling her feet back out of the slits they made each time she dug her heel in. The concentration kept her focused on maintaining her momentum, and trying to enjoy the spectacular scenery as much as possible.

Which made her slide out even more embarrassing, at least to her. Luckily, instinct took over and she threw her ax into the ice, arresting her slide immediately. "Ow!" Lana screamed automatically, though the fall onto the rough surface wasn't as bad as she'd expected. The layers of sweaters and thick winter jacket she'd bought in Reykjavik absorbed most of the fall.

When Helga whipped around to ask whether she was alright, her eyes widened and her face paled.

"Stop—that is not safe!" she screamed loudly as she rushed past them, as fast as her crampon-covered boots allowed. Lana and Willow looked back to see Audrey standing far off the path, spinning around while her friends photographed her.

Far behind them was Petur, leading the two older guests, now attached to his rope. He looked up, apparently sensing the urgency in his co-worker's voice, and also began to yell at the bachelorette party.

From where Lana was standing, she could see that the ice close to Audrey's feet was tinted blue, which according to their guides, could indicate a fissure in the glacier's surface. Helga must have noticed it, too, because she began screaming even louder and waving her hands over her head in the universal "Hey, look out" gesture.

"Why does Audrey think it's alright to leave the trail? Wasn't she listening to the safety speech?" Lana asked.

"It's like they think they are invincible! What is wrong with those girls?" Willow added.

All Lana could do was shake her head.

The wind whipping across the glacier's face was strong and seemed to blow the guide's voice away. No one in Audrey's group appeared to hear Helga calling out because the bride-to-be continued turning and twirling, giggling as she did. Only when someone in the group waved to Audrey to take a step back did the almost-bride seem to notice the guides gesturing at them.

"Do not move!" Helga screamed so loudly that Lana figured everyone on the glacier could hear her. "The ice under your feet is blue—you could be standing on the lip of a crevice. Do not back up any further," she said in a calm voice.

As a fellow tour guide, Lana could imagine that the woman was anything but relaxed on the inside. Yet, on the other hand, before boarding the minivan, they did all sign waivers releasing the company from any liability, so perhaps Helga was not as upset or edgy as she might imagine.

Audrey, however, was clearly not reassured by Helga's words or tone, for she shrieked and rushed towards her friends, still standing on the marked path.

As her feet landed on the trail, a sharp crunching noise made them all gasp. A section of ice as big as a sink broke loose and dropped into a deep rift in the ice's surface, precisely where Audrey had been standing.

"Those are the crevices I warned you about. That is exactly why I told you to stay on the trail!" Their guide was so livid she seemed to be having trouble breathing. "And where is your ice ax? I told you to keep it with you at all times!"

"But she said I could stand there because it was so close to the path. That ice did look beaten down to me." Audrey pouted as she pointed to one of the bridesmaids.

Unfortunately for Lana, the guide was standing in front of them so she couldn't see which one had given Audrey the bad advice.

"During the safety speech, I made quite clear how dangerous it is to leave the path. Why did you do the one thing I asked you specifically not to do?"

"I didn't hear everything you said because my friends were distracting me," Audrey said, already back on the offensive. Her friends kept their faces neutral, Lana assumed in a show of solidarity.

"Really?" Helga crossed her arms over her torso and looked down her nose at the bride-to-be before jerking her head towards the open fissure in the ice. "Who are you going to believe from now on—me or your friends who have never been here?"

"You." Her voice quivered and she averted her eyes before adding, "If it's so important, maybe next time you should speak more clearly. Have you considered using a megaphone?"

Their guide stared at Audrey as if she was crazy. "I have been leading groups over the ice for five years and you are the first to not hear me. Maybe you should pay more attention."

"Who does she think she is, speaking to you like that!" Tabitha exclaimed.

Yet when Helga turned and glared at the young Americans, Elaine put a hand on each of their shoulders, before either could retort.

"We'll make certain she stays with the group," Elaine said before maneuvering the pair out of their guide's sightline and towards the back.

Helga issued one final warning for everyone to stay on the trail, before working her way back to the front of the line and resuming their hike.

"I wonder which one of them told her it was okay to step off the trail. Did you catch her name?" Lana asked Willow as she glanced back at the five women.

"I did not. Did Audrey even name a person, or just point at one of her friends? I suppose it doesn't matter who told her that it was okay to do so. She's just lucky the guide reacted so quickly. You guys really have to stay on your toes, don't you?"

"Yes, sometimes being a guide does require having eyes in the back of your head." Lana laughed before adding, "Whatever happens, I hope and pray that nobody dies on this tour. My nerves are already shot, as is. And Dotty would never believe that I'm not cursed."

Willow waved her comment away. "I think she's convinced. Your recent track records of deaths threw her for a loop—"

"Heck, it threw us all for a loop, me included," Lana interjected.

"But she's put the deaths in perspective. I don't think you need to worry. Dotty is probably waiting for you to call and say you want to start leading tours again."

They were just getting back into the swing of things, when Lana glanced back and noticed the bachelorette party was dawdling again as they paused to take snapshots of each other. That in itself was not a problem, however, the young women seemed more concerned with the framing of their shots than where they were standing. Soon, they were back off the trail.

"Are you kidding me?" she muttered to Willow.

"Some people never learn," her friend replied.

When Petur began to reprimand them, the female guide held up her hand to halt their walk.

"I am sorry, everyone, but this is not safe," she called out as she passed the others again, on her way to the bachelorette party.

When she reached the young women, Helga said loudly, "I warned you already, but you refuse to listen. I insist you latch onto my rope so I can be certain you stay on the trail."

"No, we don't want to," Tabitha said, defiance in her voice.

"You walk too fast. We aren't really the outdoorsy types, as you obviously are," Destiny said, as way of explanation.

Their guide crossed her arms over her torso. "That is even more reason to take this safety precaution. You either rope up, or my colleague will escort you back to the trailhead."

"Fine by me," Tabitha grumbled.

"Me, too," Bianca agreed.

"Come on, you two. It's so pretty here," Audrey said. "And Gunnar would be disappointed if we didn't finish the hike—he said this was one of his favorite places in Iceland."

As soon as Audrey mentioned his name, it was if the tone of the conversation shifted.

"I want to see the rest of the glacier," Destiny piped up.

"Me, too," Elaine added, glaring at Tabitha and Bianca for effect. "Can't we just keep it together long enough to finish this walk?"

"It's a hike, Elaine," Tabitha hissed. "We aren't just strolling around in the park are we? Ice axes and helmets should have been your first clue."

Helga threw her hands on her hips and tried to look intimidating. "This is not a choice. We can lose our license to guide these excursions if a client gets injured through our own negligence."

Audrey tsked her tongue. "Come on, girls, stop fighting. It's my party and I say we stay. It's only going to get prettier the further we go—I'm sure of it."

Before anyone else could retort, Helga clipped the five women's harnesses onto the rope attached to her own. She turned and gently pulled them towards the front.

As the young women passed by, Lana couldn't help but think of a mother duck and her ducklings following along, single file. "I wonder if they will behave, or drag our spunky guide to her death?"

"It could go either way," Willow mumbled in response.

10

Friends in High Places

A half hour later, they reached the summit of their hike.

"Congratulations! You made it to the top of the Skaftafell Glacier! Let's take a short break and enjoy the spectacular views while we refuel our bodies. We really lucked out today with the clear weather—I haven't seen the entire Kverkfjöll mountain range in weeks," Petur enthused.

"It's best to stay standing. Trust me, if you sit down on the ice, you will regret it." Helga laughed that strange little chortle again.

Willow and Lana high-fived each other. "Yes! We did it!"

"It was tougher than I expected, but worth it. Would you look at those mountains?" Willow exclaimed.

From their perch, a small section of flattened ice near the top of the glacier, they reveled in the vast views of the tundra-like landscape spread out before them. Rising up in the distance was a scraggly mountain range, its tips lightly dusted in snow. Helga pointed out the Skarphédinstindur, the highest peak, while Petur handed out protein bars.

Destiny pushed her phone into Tabitha's hand. "Can you take a picture of me? I want to send it to Pedro. I bet he's never seen this much snow!"

"Ah yes," Tabitha smiled, "your mysterious Spanish boyfriend. I thought you two weren't in contact anymore."

Destiny's smile wavered. "Why would you think that? He can't fly over here because he's busy with university classes, that's all. We haven't broken up. I'm just going to have to fly back over there, instead. I don't own a house or have a job, so it's not like anything is keeping me in Portland."

The wind kicked up again, blowing so hard that Lana was glad she had crampons on. She ripped open her energy bar and took a large bite, in case it blew away before she could finish it.

Willow did the same, gobbling up hers in record time. "That last switchback was pretty sketchy. It felt like the wind could knock me over and back down the trail at any second."

"I know what you mean," Lana empathized as she stretched out her heel and leaned forward, attempting to alleviate the cramps forming in her calves. "Thank goodness our crampons keep us from gliding backwards or off the trail. The last thing I want to slide into is a crevice. How those bachelorettes got it into their heads to walk off the trail is beyond me. I totally get why the guide latched them all up to her rope."

She popped the last bite into her mouth, thankful for the snack. The hike was more intense than she had imagined. While it was not particularly steep, it was quite slippery, and Lana had used leg muscles she didn't even know she had, to keep her feet on the trail.

"What I still don't get is Audrey's reckless behavior. She's about to get married, for goodness' sake!" Willow said. "You would think that even if her friends said it was alright to walk off the trail, she would be smart enough to realize that it is dangerous. I wonder if she is always so flaky or if the wedding is messing with her mind."

"Audrey is pretty flaky in general, but since we arrived, she's been acting even weirder than normal," a female voice answered from behind.

Both Willow and Lana flushed pink as they turned around and discovered Elaine, the dark-haired bachelorette, standing right behind them.

Before either could apologize, Elaine continued, "You can't really blame her, though. She lives an incredibly sheltered life and has no real social skills. Considering how her aunt Maureen brought her up, I guess it is more of a shock that she is not even stranger than she already is."

Elaine regarded the topic of their conversation. "Audrey really does need a full-time guide in life. Her aunt has filled that role up until now, but as of

Friday, it will be her husband's turn."

She looked to the rest of the bachelorettes, all now free from Helga's rope, and sighed. "I hope Gunnar knows what he is getting into."

"What do you mean by sheltered? And why does Audrey live with her aunt?" Lana asked.

"It's more like Maureen lives in Audrey's house."

When Lana and Willow looked at Elaine in confusion, she added, "Audrey's parents died in a car accident when she was five years old. They were really well-off and left their mansion and everything else they owned to Audrey, which is why her aunt moved into the family's home and raised her there. Her aunt's nice enough, but overly protective, if you ask me."

Elaine glanced up at the other bachelorettes, as if to ensure none were close enough to hear her, before she added softly, "Audrey's parents died in a drinking and driving accident, and the rumor is, her dad was the one who caused it. But that's never been confirmed by the media or police. Either way, her aunt seems to believe it. It's almost like she is afraid that Audrey will immediately succumb to bad influences, if left to her own devices."

"Is her aunt flying over for the wedding?" Lana shifted uncomfortably on her feet.

Elaine grimaced. "No, they had a pretty nasty argument right before Audrey left, and she refused to tell her aunt when or where they are getting married. Not that she would have to do much to find out where it is taking place—it's big news back home, these two rich families joining together in matrimony."

"What did her parents do to become so wealthy?"

"They were computer programmers and they had founded several startups that are now worth millions. They put all of their money, stocks, and control of their businesses into a sort of trust fund. When Audrey turns twenty-five or gets married, she will become the CEO of all of the companies—at least on paper. And she'll finally have direct access to her family's bank accounts, something she has been dying to get her hands on. She receives a healthy monthly allowance as it is, but it never seems to be enough for her."

Elaine regarded the bachelorette party again. "Or at least, not enough to pay for everything she and her friends want. She does have a lot of people hanging on her coattails."

"What do you mean?"

She leaned in closer. "Take Tabitha. That's her shopping buddy, but somehow Audrey ends up paying for everything they leave the store with."

"Does her aunt know?" Willow asked.

"I think she turns a blind eye. Tabitha's mom is one of her best friends, at least currently. Otherwise, she would do everything she could to forbid Audrey from buying her things. They might be rich, but Maureen keeps a close eye on Audrey's spending. But then again, Tabitha is so manipulative, Audrey might not even be aware that's she's always picking up the bills."

Lana frowned at Elaine's choice of words. "What do you mean Tabitha's mom and Audrey's aunt are currently friends? Did something happen recently that might affect their friendship?"

Elaine chortled. "You could say that. I truly wonder if Tabitha's mom will still talk to Maureen after Audrey's wedding."

"What an odd thing to say—is she against their union? Or is Tabitha also interested in Gunnar?" Willow asked, clearly as intrigued as Lana was.

"No, but both Tabitha and her mom worship wealth and status most of all. Once Audrey marries, Maureen won't have as much money to toss around. As Audrey's caretaker, she has been receiving a monthly stipend as a sort of payment for taking care of her niece. But after the wedding, she'll only receive a fraction of that amount. I doubt she'll be able to afford her country club membership, which will make her less interesting to several of her current friends. They really are an exclusive group."

Lana frowned. "Not to be rude, but this seems like personal information. How do you know so much about Audrey's family and financial situation?"

Elaine laughed. "I guess it is personal, but you don't know Audrey. Talking about money is one of her favorite pastimes, along with hanging out at 'the club,' riding her horses, and shopping 'til she drops. That's pretty much all that makes her world go round. Which means I might have been too hard on Tabitha. She just might be the person who understands Audrey the best. Tabitha does love money, shopping, and horses as much as Audrey does. Though I don't know if they are riding together as often, since Audrey started hanging out with Bianca."

"Bianca is the maid of honor, right? How do she and Audrey know each other?" Willow asked.

"Her uncle owns the stable where Audrey keeps her horse. Bianca's family is famous for breeding racehorses, and they have stables in Portland and San Francisco. Audrey's aunt suggested the two ride together, and soon enough they became buddies. Bianca might be a true friend to her, but I don't know her well enough. She doesn't like me much, but that's because Audrey and I spend time together, too. Bianca seems to be jealous of anyone else who gets too close to Audrey. I bet that's why she's been acting superior to Tabitha and Destiny all week. Her being the maid of honor has become a point of pride."

Elaine's true feelings for Bianca came to the surface and soon she was spitting her words out. "Rumor has it that Bianca made a move on Gunnar at a party a few months ago. Some say he rejected her flat-out, but a trusted source saw him leaving her place the next morning. Personally, I don't believe they did spend the night together. Gunnar barely tolerates Bianca, from what I can see. Either way, Audrey doesn't know about it yet, and I am fairly certain someone is going to slip up before the week is through and mention it. And once Audrey finds out, that might be the end of Gunnar. She doesn't like leftovers."

Elaine looked again to her travel companions before adding, "Which is why Audrey doesn't want her friends to know that he and Destiny went out a few times."

"They did? And yet she's one of Audrey's bridesmaids. Geez, they must really be good friends."

"Yeah, well, from what I understand, it wasn't serious, which is probably the only reason why Audrey still talks to her. Destiny's family is well off, but not super rich like Gunnar and Audrey are, and people like that tend to stick together. When Destiny went to Europe for the summer, Audrey and Gunnar hooked up. And three months later, they were engaged!"

"Wow, that was really fast. They must have a lot in common. How did

Destiny react?" Willow asked.

"Better than I expected. She had met a Spanish guy during her travels and was still in contact with him after they got back. However, from what Audrey told me, it petered out pretty fast, once Destiny made clear she expected him to fly over to see her. Apparently he is a student and can't afford to fly over to America right now—at least, that's what he told her."

"That's too bad."

Elaine shrugged. "Vacation romances usually aren't meant to last. We let our inhibitions go, once we are out of our comfort zone." She turned red and laughed. "Just like me now, telling you and Willow all about us. I don't know a thing about either one of you, except that Lana was once a tour guide."

"Still am." She held up her hand. "But even tour guides need to take a vacation now and again."

As obvious as it was that Elaine was dying to spread gossip about her supposed friends, Lana wasn't that interested in hearing all of the nitty-gritty details of their privileged lives. Unsure how to end the conversation, she stamped her feet and looked out over the valley below, hoping Elaine would wander back to her friends. The sun peeking through the clouds warmed the ice enough to make the top layer soft, but did little to heat up their bodies. Standing still here on the ice's surface was beginning to feel like standing inside of a freezer.

Willow, on the other hand, was apparently too curious to let it go. "Yikes. That's pretty risky then, you all being together for a whole week. We did notice Destiny, Bianca, and Tabitha flirting with Gunnar at breakfast the other day, but thought we were imagining things. I hope for Audrey's sake that they'll leave him alone once they're hitched."

"I'm sure it will be an adjustment for both of them, being joined together in matrimony. But then again, I wouldn't be surprised to learn that Audrey is marrying him more to get away from her aunt, than because she is in love with him. Maybe she'll let his indiscretions slide."

"She wouldn't be the first person to do so," Willow said sympathetically.

The more they learned about Audrey, the sadder her life seemed to be. She wasn't at all the image Lana had had of a young heir to a vast fortune. Hoping to move the conversation back to the lighter side, she asked in a teasing tone, "Is Destiny a shopping buddy or a horse lover?"

"She's a neighbor and a homeschool buddy. Both were taught by private tutors so Maureen and Destiny's mom arranged weekly playdates for them, to help them socialize. Unfortunately, Destiny has always been extremely jealous of Audrey, which makes them more frenemies than actual friends, in my opinion. But who am I to judge? Audrey doesn't seem to notice, and I bet if you asked Destiny, she would tell you that they are best friends. But from what Audrey's told me, they've always been in competition with each other."

Elaine checked to ensure the four blondes were still standing far enough away not to hear, before adding, "It didn't help that their fathers also used to work together, but they got into a fight, and Destiny's dad quit a few weeks before Audrey's parents were killed in that car crash. From what I understand, Destiny's dad was never as successful as Audrey's dad. That might be where Destiny's competitiveness comes from."

Lana regarded Elaine critically. She didn't get the impression that the younger woman was a close friend of Audrey's, but she sure did know a lot about the bride-to-be and her friends.

"And how do you know Audrey?"

"Technically, I work for her, or at least for the estate. I'm one of the gardeners. My mother used to work for them as a housecleaner, and when the assistant gardener's position opened up, she suggested me."

"I didn't expect that," Lana blurted out, then covered her mouth in embarrassment. How did one of the family's gardeners end up as one of the bridesmaids?

Elaine's laugh set her at ease. "It's okay. I'm not a horse lover, shopper, or member of the country club, which are the usual ways Audrey meets people. I realize me being here sounds strange, but Audrey's only four years younger than me and didn't have many opportunities to meet other people her own age. When I started working on the grounds, she was still being homeschooled. Whenever she took a break from her lessons, she would come out into the garden and find me for a chat. I think she enjoyed talking to another teenager, or at least a female closer to her age. All of her tutors were retired professors, so they really didn't get our generation."

"That's really sweet," Willow said.

Elaine scratched her cheek. "To be honest, it made me uncomfortable at first, but my mom had asked me to talk to her, out of politeness. Audrey has never had many friends because her aunt kept her away from most social events where she could actually meet people her own age. I hate horses and shop as little as possible, so we don't have anything in common, but we get along well enough."

"And as for money…" Elaine chuckled before continuing, "For a middle-class family with three kids, we have a pretty big house. When Audrey came over to visit for the first and last time, she expressed her shock that a family could live in something so small and then left before my mom could pour her a cup of tea. Mom was so offended, she told me to call in sick for a whole week! But I knew that Audrey didn't mean to be cruel. She just doesn't have any social skills. In my book, that's her aunt's fault, not Audrey's."

Lana shifted on her heel. Elaine's tone was turning dark again. "That must be fun, being a gardener and making things grow," she said. Even to Lana's ears, her words sounded lame.

Elaine snorted. "If only it were that easy. Most of the time I'm worrying about getting stung by nettles, loose branches falling on my head, the lawn mower breaking down again, getting legionella—the list goes on. It's not really my calling, but I didn't have much choice. I struggled to finish high school and didn't want to go to university. But Dad said I had to either learn a skill or move out. When he suggested this training program, I immediately agreed. It was offered close to home and only took a year to complete."

"A year—to be a gardener!" Lana blurted out, then immediately regretted her choice of words.

"Technically, I am a horticulturist. I hope to own my own landscape design company, one day. Besides, gardening is not just knowing what to cut back and when, but also how to recognize weakness and infestations, and knowing how to remedy them. At my school, they emphasized using naturally occurring pesticides and biocontrol, instead of chemicals."

Afraid of making another blunder, Lana remained silent.

Elaine apparently took that as a sign that she was uncomfortable, because she quickly added, "Just so you don't get the wrong idea, I am fond of Audrey. Heck, I might even be the closest thing she's got to a true friend, seeing as I may be the only person on this planet that doesn't want anything from her. But I'm still very much the help. Honestly, if she hadn't read in her favorite magazine that you need at least three bridesmaids at your wedding, I doubt she would have asked me."

"She doesn't have any other close friends?" Willow uttered.

"Not really. She spends all her time on horses and shopping. I've never heard her express any ambition to do anything else with her life. And those hobbies limit the amount of new people you meet."

Lana was shocked by how forthcoming Elaine was with these rather negative things about her supposed friends. On the other hand, she didn't seem to be smitten with anyone in the bachelorette party. Was she simply feeling left out because she was poor in comparison to her traveling companions? Or was there something else going on?

11

One Problem Resolved

Before Lana could try to find out, Helga clapped her hands together. "I bet you are getting cold! Why don't we start walking and warm up again."

"I can't feel my feet," Lana confided.

"My face is freezing," Willow added, briskly rubbing her gloved hands against her cheeks for emphasis. The walking kept their body temperature up, but now that they'd stopped, Lana's blood felt as if it was turning to ice.

Audrey's group stopped posing for photos and put their phones away, before allowing Helga to tether them to her rope again.

"Shoot—I forgot to take a picture!" Lana whipped her phone out and snapped a few selfies, as well as shots of the summit and Willow, before they joined the line of hikers already descending the glacier.

The hike down went much quicker than their slow walk up the ice field. Lana tempered her steps and concentrated on keeping her heel firmly planted, out of fear of her crampons sliding her down the mountain like ice skates.

Once they made it down the glacier, their group removed their gear and thanked their guides for leading the hike. As soon as they were seated, the awaiting Jeeps set off towards the parking lot. Lana was almost lulled into sleep by the vehicle's motions before they made it back to their tour bus.

Luckily the few minutes of complete relaxation reenergized her because, based on their tour guide's bouncy movements, she had a feeling they wouldn't be able to rest during the ride to their hotel.

"Did you enjoy your hike?" she asked the bachelorettes as they trailed into the bus, clearly expecting an outpouring of enthusiastic reactions. Bianca, Destiny, and Tabitha walked silently past as if she had not spoken.

"It was nice," Audrey answered, though her expression was anything but enthusiastic.

"But it was more of a hike than we had expected. I think we are all pretty tired," Elaine rushed to add—out of politeness, Lana figured. She really was the only one who seemed to show strangers any modicum of respect. Was it because Elaine was not as wealthy as the others? Audrey and her rich friends did seem to see themselves as better than the rest.

What a shame, Lana thought. She had dealt with enough wealthy older clients on her tours to know that money did not always make a person happy. It must be even stranger to be so young and so well off. What would their purpose in life be? For most, it was to educate yourself so you could find a good job and eventually buy a house. But if everything was provided for a person at such an early age, what would motivate them to get out of the bed in the morning?

When she and Willow passed their guide on the way into the bus, both made a point of telling her how wonderful the hike was. "I've never seen anything like it before," Willow gushed, leaving the guide beaming with pride.

"Well, tomorrow you are in for another treat. Our first stop will be Gullfoss Waterfall, one of the most famous in Iceland."

"That does sound spectacular," Lana agreed as her stomach began to rumble. Her body had already used up the energy provided by that protein bar on the summit. "Not to be rude, but are we going to have dinner at the hotel? Or could you recommend a restaurant in town?"

Willow's eyes grew wide as she grinned at Lana. "Somebody didn't read the itinerary."

Lana blushed at her friend's whispered comment, embarrassed that Willow had caught her out. At least now she understood why some of her own clients preferred to rely on the guide instead of consulting the provided itinerary.

"No problem, that's what I'm here for. We do have reservations at our hotel's restaurant, which is one of the best in Vik. As soon as we get there, I can ask that they serve dinner immediately."

"That would be wonderful."

Their guide nodded and smiled demurely as the pair passed.

When they took their seats again, Willow leaned over to Lana. "How does it feel, to not know what's going on every minute of the day?"

"Pretty nice, actually. It's quite freeing to live in the moment. I'll have to remember that the next time a client relies on me to tell them what's going on, instead of consulting the itinerary."

Willow squeezed her shoulder. "I'm glad to hear you say that. You're an excellent tour guide and I know you will continue to be."

"That's not what I meant—" Lana started to correct her friend, then stopped. In her long list of short-lived careers and professions, leading tours was her favorite job by a long shot. And it was not one that she was ready to give up on quite yet.

"I guess I'll have to call Dotty when we get back to Reykjavik."

"I think that's a great idea," Willow said, adding with a laugh, "As long as no one dies on this tour, you're a shoo-in."

One problem resolved, Lana thought as she laughed along. *Now all I have to do is figure out what to do about Alex.*

12

Baby Talk

Wednesday—Day Two of the Southern Island Tour of Iceland

After a lovely dinner, Lana and Willow had each taken a bath and then passed out in their hotel room. To make up for not exploring Vik the night before, they had tried to take a short walk around the old village before breakfast, but their guide caught them leaving and rushed them into the breakfast room, instead.

Once everyone was seated, she clapped her hands together, ensuring everyone was paying attention.

"We have a busy day today. I'm sorry to say that you only have thirty minutes to eat breakfast, then we need to board the bus. The good news is, our early departure means we might have the Gullfoss Falls for ourselves!"

Lana didn't mind the pep talk so early in the morning, but the chipper clapping did grate on her nerves.

"When we get to Gullfoss, we are going to have a picnic lunch close to the trailhead, before we hike over to the waterfall. Our chefs have prepared a wonderful selection of Icelandic favorites for us to enjoy while we take in the stunning views."

"Sounds great," Lana answered and shuffled over to the breakfast buffet.

It was a few hours' drive to the waterfall, and Lana and Willow spent their time chatting about mutual friends Lana hadn't seen in far too long. Because she had been working back-to-back tours for several months, she hadn't been home for more than a few days since the start of the year. *I really should take a week off and go back to Seattle, before resuming my tour duties,* Lana thought.

Too soon, their bus was pulling into another parking lot and their guide was rising to grab the microphone.

"Time to wake up, sleepyheads," she said in a teasing voice, causing the bachelorette party to stretch.

"Man, I haven't slept that soundly in months," Audrey said before yawning loudly. "It must be thanks to that great workout."

"Me, either. It sure beats Pilates. Too bad we don't have many hikeable glaciers close to Portland," Destiny added.

"I wonder if there are year-round glaciers on Mount Hood. It would be worth finding out," Elaine added.

"Are you kidding me? The last thing I want to do is hike another glacier. That crampon sliced through my pants leg. It's a good thing this was a gift from Gunnar, otherwise I would have made those Ice Masters pay for a new pair," Tabitha said.

"I hope we don't have to walk far this time. My legs are already cramping up," Bianca added.

Lana and Willow rolled their eyes at each other.

"I wonder what trouble they are going to get into this time," Willow whispered, getting a giggle out of Lana.

"Great question. At least we don't have to worry about them falling into crevices during this hike."

Their guide ushered them out of the vehicle and then pointed to a small gravel path at the far end of the parking lot.

"That's the trail to a fantastic viewpoint overlooking the lower falls. Before we hike over there, we are going to have a picnic lunch over on that field." She pointed to a patch of grass directly next to the trailhead. It appeared to be on a rocky cliff that jutted out over the fast-moving river, deep in the valley below.

Their guide pulled two large picnic blankets out from under the bus, and the driver grabbed several baskets of food. Before setting off towards the grass, she added, "From our picnic spot, you will be able to see the Hvítá River and the lower falls. While we are setting up lunch, why don't you enjoy the views? Please don't go too far down the trail just yet—it would be a shame to waste all of this delicious food!"

Willow and Lana didn't need to be told twice. The thundering roar of the waterfall drew the two women towards the water. They wandered a ways down the gravel trail, ensuring they stayed close enough to hear their guide. The narrow path followed a wide ledge of stone that paralleled the river. Even after walking only a few feet, they could see the entire waterfall. It was much wider than she had expected and the drops far higher. The water thundered over the rocks with such force, it created a thick layer of mist that enshrouded the pools below. The sound of pure energy was mesmerizing.

Lana could tell where the water and spray landed most often, simply because those patches of earth and stone were covered with a lush layer of grass and moss. Those green areas were in stark contrast with the otherwise rocky gray-brown walls of stone that contained the waterfall and river.

The two friends stared at the cascading streams of frothy water tumbling over the large stone slabs. Instead of one fall, Gullfoss was a series of drops that made a sharp turn in the middle, reminding Lana of a staircase twisting around a corner.

Suddenly Willow grabbed ahold of her and pulled her close, hugging her tight. "I am so glad to be here, sharing this experience with you."

Startled by the emotion in her friend's voice, Lana hugged her back before gently pulling away and examining Willow's face. The tears forming in her eyes confirmed Lana's suspicions. "I'm so glad you came over, but I can't shake the feeling that there is something you aren't telling me. Are you doing alright?"

Willow blushed and shoved her hands in her pockets. "I'm not keeping anything from you. It's just… I know I'm not supposed to say this, but it's so good just to be Willow for a few days, instead of Zoe's mom. I don't mean to sound ungrateful—Zoe is the best thing that's ever happened to me. But it takes a lot out of a person, caring for another living being. There is always this underlying worry that she's putting a magnet in her mouth or climbing up the stairs backwards again. It messes with you mentally."

"I bet," Lana said in her most sympathetic tone. Because she did not have children, she shied away from offering any advice with regard to their care. "You know that I don't know much about having a kid, but I do know that they grow up pretty fast. Maybe it's a phase?"

Willow shook her head. "If it's not marbles, it'll be her choice of date or clothing that keeps me up at night. But I signed up for that when I had her; I know that. It's just far more intense than I could have imagined."

Lana nodded. "Is it just being a mom that's getting you down, or is there something else?"

Willow sighed and momentarily stared off into the fast-moving river before answering. "I also miss giving lessons and interacting with my clients. I know I shouldn't complain—it was my choice to stay home with her instead of putting her in day care. And Jane is the most supportive partner, and a wonderful parent. She offered to work four days a week after Zoe was born, but I turned her down. In hindsight, I really regret that decision."

"I think every mother questions her decisions and wonders if she is doing it right or if she should have done something differently. From what I can see, Zoe is a wonderfully happy, and most definitely loved, little girl. That's all that matters."

Lana paused, wondering whether she dared to continue speaking her mind. But it was her best friend, so she decided to be as candid as she could. "Is that decision—that you stay at home and Jane work full time—irreversible? If Jane isn't able to rearrange her schedule, maybe you could look for a day care?"

Lana knew she had to tread carefully—the waiting lists for the better day cares were usually so long, the child would often be in third grade before there was a spot for them.

"No and yes," Willow answered with a laugh. "I was the one who saw everything as set in stone, but Jane had already talked it over with her partners, and they were open to changing the schedule so she could be home more. I'm the one who said it wasn't necessary."

"You're a grown woman and are allowed to change your mind."

"I know, but having to ask her to help out more feels like I failed. I was so determined to do it all myself. But now that I'm here and have a little distance, I realize it's my pride that's preventing me from broaching the subject again. It's like having to admit that I'm not Superwoman, after all."

"I don't know, you're pretty magical to me! I seriously don't know how you do it. Your business is flourishing, your relationship with your wife is stronger than ever, and your daughter is one of the sweetest babies I've ever met."

"Says her godmother," Willow added with a chuckle.

"But why wait to talk to Jane? She already offered to work a day less; why not take her up on it? Then you could be more active in your own company again. And it would be good for Jane to have some time alone with Zoe. At least, that's what all the magazines say about bonding with your babies," Lana rushed to add, unsure whether she had crossed a line.

Willow reflected a moment. "I don't know what's stopping me, actually. I suppose I don't have to wait, do I?"

"Let's be honest, Jane must know you are itching to be back in your studio again." Willow was the owner of Willows Bend Yoga Studio, where the pair had met after Lana hurt her shoulder and used yoga to rehabilitate it.

Willow chuckled. "You're right. It was gut-wrenching to have to hire another teacher last month, but I didn't have a choice. The new Zumba and kickboxing classes are incredibly popular and have waiting lists. That's another thing that's been bothering me. I used to know all of my regular clients, but now, when I pop in to pick up paperwork or drop off checks, I hardly recognize anyone! I feel like a stranger in my own studio, and I don't like it."

"That's it—you have to talk to Jane."

Willow nodded, now with more enthusiasm. "I really do. Come to think of it, there's a day care opening close to my house. Since it's new, it shouldn't have a horribly long waiting list, especially for only one or two days. It might be good for both me and Zoe to socialize with our peers. And if Jane can carve out a mama day, that would give me a few days to teach classes."

Lana squeezed her friend's arm and opened her mouth to respond when their guide waved and then yelled out, "The picnic lunch is ready. I hope you will join us!" She pointed towards two bright-red picnic blankets covered in a plethora of food. The rest of the guests were already sampling the many dishes.

"Are you hungry?" Lana asked.

"I wasn't until she asked, but now I am," Willow admitted. "Shall we join them for lunch?"

"Sounds good to me."

13

A Close Call

As much as Lana and Willow tried to avoid the bachelorette party, the small size of their group meant they were continually crossing paths. When they approached the picnic blankets, the only places left to sit were across from the five young women. Just as they were about to take their places, Audrey stood up.

"Where's the bathroom? I want to wash my hands."

"There aren't any facilities here, so our bus is the best option. If you knock on the door, the driver will let you in."

"Okay, see you in a minute," Audrey called out as she scurried to the bus.

Before either Lana or Willow could examine all of the dishes laid out on the blanket, Tabitha spoke up, adding an unexpected twist to the afternoon. "Gunnar's right, Audrey is getting fat."

Lana shook her head, certain she'd heard Tabitha wrong. Audrey was not anorexic-thin, but she couldn't be larger than a size four.

"It's probably all the extra food she's been eating that's been messing with her insulin," Bianca said.

"She has swollen right up. I bet she won't fit into her wedding dress on Friday if she keeps it up," Destiny added.

Tabitha sniggered. "I hope not—she promised me the dress if she got too fat for it. That's why I've been encouraging her to sample everything."

"Oh, you dog, you!" Bianca slapped her hand and laughed.

Tabitha lowered her voice to a conspiratorial whisper that was audible to all. "Come on, she's rich enough to buy something at the last minute if she wants to. I bet Gunnar knows some hip Icelandic fashion diva who could whip something up for Audrey, as long as she pays through the nose for it."

"It's all about the money with those two, isn't it? I bet that's why Gunnar proposed so quickly. He met his match, qua checkbook," Bianca speculated.

"Audrey swept him off his feet, just like Pedro did to me. Sometimes you don't need to know someone for long to know they are the right person for you," Destiny said.

"True love or not, if she can't fit into that Vera Wang dress on Friday, Gunnar's going to throw a hissy fit," Bianca said. "We'd better keep her away from the sweet stuff for the rest of the week."

"That's going to be a challenge—did you see how she wolfed down those three chocolate croissants after Gunnar left the hotel?" Tabitha cackled.

"They really are the true definition of 'frenemy,'" Willow whispered to Lana, who nodded emphatically.

"You guys are terrible!" Elaine screeched, echoing the pair's thoughts. "Audrey finally meets the man of her dreams and all you can talk about is how fat she is?"

A choked sob made the bachelorettes turn. Audrey stood a few feet behind them, and based on the tears running down her cheeks, she had heard every word. "Elaine was right; you are all using me. None of you are my real friends!"

"Of course we are, Audrey," Bianca soothed. "We would do anything for you! It's Elaine you should watch out for. She can't keep her eyes off Gunnar."

"Are you kidding me? I am not interested in your fiancé, Audrey."

"They do say opposites attract," Tabitha added.

"Gunnar is the one with a wandering eye; I didn't encourage him. But I've never taken him up on his many offers—have any of you?" When Elaine turned to glare at the three blondes, the trio acted as if they were shocked by her suggestion.

"How dare you!" Audrey threw her hands on her hips and glared at Elaine. "If my fiancé is such a skirt-chaser, why didn't you say something before we flew over here? Heck, why didn't you say anything when I told you we were engaged?"

When Elaine stared down at the ground instead of meeting Audrey's eye, the almost-bride raged on. "If you really are my friend and if what you say is true, then you would have told me about him being unfaithful. So I have to conclude that you are not my friend and are lying about Gunnar. I don't want to see you anymore."

"Wait—are you uninviting me to your wedding?" Elaine's head flew back, as if Audrey had slapped her.

"You're making a wise choice," Tabitha enthused as she sprung up and tried to wrap her arm around the bride-to-be's shoulders.

Audrey jerked away. "That is exactly what I am doing, Elaine. But I heard what you said about me, Tabitha. Seriously—you were trying to fatten me up for a dress? It's my wedding! Don't I buy enough clothes for you? None of you are acting like friends. I don't want to see any of you right now."

Audrey turned away from the picnic and galloped off down the path leading to the lower falls. Tears flew from her cheeks as she went.

"Audrey—stop! We love you—don't go!" Bianca cried out and raced after her. Tabitha and Destiny chased after them, too, but at a far slower pace. Elaine stayed where she was, staring at the ground and looking dejected.

"What a drama," Lana said to her friend.

"Tensions sure are running high with that bunch," Willow remarked as she watched the trio of blondes trail after Audrey.

After the last blonde bridesmaid was out of sight, Willow made a show of looking over the selection of fruits, breads, salads, cold cuts, and cheeses. "So, what should we sample first?"

Lana startled at her friend's casual attitude. "What about Audrey?"

"What about her? She's got a crew of women to look after her, as well as our guide. You're on vacation, remember? There's no need to get involved." Willow picked up two plates and handed one to Lana, as if emphasizing what her choice was.

Lana looked over at the guide, who was staring down the trail leading to the base of the waterfall. She could almost sense her confusion and hesitation.

Should she run after her guests, or attend to the rest? How many times had she been in the same situation on one of her Wanderlust tours, Lana wondered. This was exactly the sort of situation that required two guides; she realized, it was sad to see this Icelandic company had sent only one along.

"I better go and check on the others. Can you please stay here and enjoy your lunch? If you need anything, ask the bus driver. I'll be right back." Their guide smiled nervously before jogging down the trail.

Lana nodded, knowing she would have gone after Audrey, as well. It wasn't a guide's place to put themselves in between two fighting clients, but it was important to ensure that everyone stayed safe. And the members of the bridal party were not particularly sporty, nor did the women have the common sense to stay on the trail.

Yet today, Lana was not the guide, but simply a tourist. The urge to get involved passed as quickly as it surfaced, and she decided to be like Willow and focus on the food instead of the other guests.

She took the plate from her friend's hand and was scooping up a serving of seafood salad, when a terrified scream pierced the air, causing her to drop her plate. The sound of ceramic shattering reverberated through the air as she tore down the path, Willow right behind her. As much as she didn't care for the women, the sound of someone in need of help affected her primally. She simply couldn't ignore such a cry.

As they rushed along the slippery path, Lana looked back towards the picnic blankets and noted that the rest of the group were also following the screams towards the base of the waterfall. Elaine must be in really good shape, she figured, because the bachelorette managed to race past the rest and quickly caught up with Lana and Willow just as another yell, this one even more soul-wrenching, echoed over the curvy trail.

"Is that Audrey calling out?" Lana asked.

"I think so. But I don't see her on the viewing platform," Elaine said as they rounded a bend and the end of the trail came into view. They both looked ahead towards the massive boulder, its surface so flat, it was as if someone had taken a chisel to it. The makeshift platform jutted over the last fall, just before the water careened over the edge and into a large basin of churning water, far below. Lana shivered, thinking about how cold that water would be.

She squinted, but couldn't see Audrey either. Only Bianca was standing on the rocky platform. The way she frantically searched the water caused Lana's stomach to knot up. Their guide, Tabitha, and Destiny had almost reached her, but the slipperiness of the trail was clearly slowing them down.

All of a sudden, Bianca rushed to one edge and crouched onto her knees before leaning down into the water. There were no railings, and the surface glistened with spray.

"That doesn't look safe," Lana muttered.

"What is Bianca doing?" Elaine wondered aloud.

The wind whipped past them, bringing droplets of ice-cold water and Audrey's cries with it. "Help me!" For a brief second, Audrey's hand was visible over the side of the rocky edge just in front of Bianca, but disappeared again.

"Oh, no, did Audrey fall in?" Elaine cried, before tearing off towards the boulder, Lana and Willow hot on her heels.

Once they reached the platform, the sound of the water pounding over the rocks overwhelmed her. Lana stepped carefully across the large slab of rock, slippery wet with mud and spray. From here, she could see Audrey's legs submerged in the fast-moving water, and the undercurrent seemed to be pulling her down. Her fingers were wrapped around a jagged stone jutting out of the side, but everything glistened with water from the heavy spray raining down on them. There was no way Audrey could hold on for long.

Audrey turned and looked at the strong currents, screaming again. "I can't feel my legs! Someone—please help me!"

"Hang on, Audrey," their guide screamed as she rushed across the boulder towards her client. As they watched, Bianca leaned farther over the rocky edge, but couldn't quite reach Audrey's hand. Their guide, however, was able to grab ahold of her wrist. Together, she and Bianca pulled her up and onto the boulder. Audrey wrapped her arms around the guide's legs, crying as she shivered terribly.

Lana felt a wave of relief wash over her when she realized how close Audrey had come to being swept away. She turned to Willow and hugged her friend tight.

By the time she and Willow reached Audrey, the rest of the bachelorette party had encircled the bride-to-be and were rubbing her shoulders and stroking her hair.

"So cold." Audrey's teeth chattered so badly, Lana could barely understand her. Their guide was already whipping silver blankets out of her daypack and wrapping them around her wet client.

"We need to get her back to the bus. Can you walk?"

Audrey attempted to nod, but her head bobbed around in a circle instead. The four bachelorettes lifted their friend up, wrapping their arms around her for support and warmth. Slowly, they made their way back up the trail and to the bus.

Once they helped her change into dry clothes, the guide sat across from Audrey. "You are quite lucky. The water temperature is so cold, I'm surprised hypothermia hasn't kicked in. Can you tell me what happened?"

"I was so angry, I wasn't looking at where I was going. Then I heard Bianca close behind me. When I turned around to look, I must have slipped and hit my head because it really hurts." Audrey gently touched the back of her skull, as if for emphasis. "The next thing I knew, I was in the water. I grabbed onto a rock that was jutting out, but it was so slippery it was hard to hang on. And then I saw Bianca there, trying to help me back up."

"I only wish I could have reached your hand," Bianca said as she looked to the ground.

Audrey smiled radiantly up at her maid of honor. "Seeing you there, trying so hard to reach me, it gave me the strength to hang on."

Bianca embraced her friend. "I'm so glad! I really thought you were a goner."

"And the rest of you ran down to help me, too." She gazed up at Tabitha, Elaine, and Destiny as the three moved in to hug Audrey, as well. The bride-to-be welcomed them with open arms. "I misjudged you. You really are my friends. I'm sorry I was so upset with you."

"It's just the stress of travel and your upcoming wedding," Destiny soothed.

"We understand," Elaine added.

"It's only natural for us all to be a little on edge," Tabitha agreed.

Their guide gazed at the five women, now wrapped up in a group hug. "You are quite lucky to have such good friends, Audrey."

14

Baseball Bats

After the guests helped their guide bring all of the picnic supplies into the vastly warmer bus, the small group seemed to get along better than they had earlier in the tour. Between bites, guests took turns swapping silly stories about previous travel mishaps they had been involved with, many bringing tears of laughter to both Willow and Lana's eyes. Although she felt no need to share her own horror stories, Lana did enjoy listening to the others regale them with their adventures.

After they had eaten and the color had come back into Audrey's cheeks, their guide approached the bachelorette party.

"That was quite the fall. I'm glad to see that you are feeling better, Audrey. Would you like to join us on our next excursion, or would you prefer to go to the hotel?"

"I can't take another hike," Destiny stated. "I can't believe Gunnar thought we would like this outdoorsy stuff."

"Count me out," Tabitha agreed. "That glacier was so icy and cold. This is not my idea of fun."

"Isn't that the definition of a glacier, that it be icy and cold?" Willow quipped.

Lana stifled a giggle. Luckily, they were seated far enough away that the bachelorettes couldn't hear them whispering.

"I didn't sign up for crevices and icy paths of mud. Is he trying to get us killed?" Bianca moaned. "He should have known that this was not our kind of thing."

Lana couldn't tell whether the women were simply releasing stress by complaining, or if they were focusing on the inherent dangers of the hikes to keep their minds off Audrey's near-fatal accident.

"Gunnar just wanted me to learn more about the land he comes from and thought you all would enjoy it, too. Obviously not." Audrey rubbed her side and thighs. "I hope our hotel has a spa because all I want to do for the rest of the day is relax in a jacuzzi. Sorry, but I'm done with hiking for the day."

"That's alright. Considering the nasty fall you took, it might be best to stay in and unwind this afternoon," the guide replied. "But I do hope you can join us for dinner. It's a special meal of puffin, and many guests say it is one of the highlights of the tour."

"I'd like to try it," Elaine said, "but only if Audrey is up for it. Can we decide later and let you know?"

"Of course." Their guide smiled at the group before walking up to the driver and relaying their revised plans.

When the bus's engine started up, Tabitha said, "I hope you two are going somewhere warmer for your honeymoon."

"We are," Audrey replied, a dreamy lilt to her voice. "Gunnar has planned out a tour of southern Europe. I can't wait to see Spain. You're lucky to have spent so much time there last summer, Destiny. It looks amazing."

"It really is. The architecture is beautiful, and the tapas are to die for."

"Where are you most excited about seeing, Audrey?" Tabitha asked.

"The Alhambra—it looks magical."

"I would love to visit it one day," Destiny said, her tone just as dreamy as Audrey's.

Elaine frowned. "You were in Spain for the summer and you didn't go to the Alhambra? I thought it was one of the most visited destinations in Spain."

"Of course we tried to see it, but we were rushed and the tickets were sold out," Destiny stammered. "I'm saving it for next time. Did you know they sell out days in advance? I hope Gunnar has ordered tickets for you."

"I'm certain he has. Gunnar is so wonderfully organized, unlike me,"

Audrey giggled. Her laugh turned to a yawn, and soon she was stretching her arms out over her head.

"Can I take a nap on the way to the hotel? That fall really wore me out. All I want to do is crash out on the seats at the back."

"Of course, Audrey," Tabitha murmured. "We'll move up to the front, to give you more space."

As Audrey made her way towards them, Willow and Lana gathered up their things so that she could stretch out on the long row of seats lining the rear of the bus.

"Hey Audrey, how are you feeling?" Lana asked.

"Like someone beat me up with a baseball bat," Audrey admitted. "Thanks for giving up your seats for me. I really need to rest."

15

A Family Visit

After they dropped the bachelorette party off at the hotel by Lake Hidavatu, the driver whisked the rest off to the last stop of the day. The hotel was farther away than Lana had expected, meaning their tour of the Geysir geothermal area was delayed by two hours. Still, it gave them enough time to see it all. The walk through the multitude of geysers and craters bubbling and boiling all over the place reminded her of the surface of the moon. The bleak nature of the place was even stranger, considering they were surrounded by rolling hills covered in grass and trees.

After a long day of hikes, Lana and Willow were ready to take a break once they got back to the hotel. However, when they entered the lobby, they walked straight into a catfight between Audrey and an older woman dressed in an expensive suit and high heels that were not at all appropriate for Iceland. From the expressions of astonishment on the faces of everyone in the lobby, the show had just begun.

"How did you find me?" Audrey cried.

"Your credit card's transactions. That led me to the hotel in Reykjavik, and they told me you were on this tour."

"You had no right—that's my personal credit card!"

The older lady's eyes narrowed. "I pay the bills, remember? I have the right to do whatever I want."

"Not for long." Audrey crossed her arms over her torso and smiled

82

wickedly.

The woman's face drained of color. "You didn't …"

"Oh yes, I did. I warned you—if you tried to stand in my way, I would go around you."

"But you are so young. If it is true love, then it won't matter if you wait. He's only rushing you into marriage so he can get his hands on your money. I bet it's his father's doing."

"His family is rich—richer than I am."

"No they aren't—it's all a lie, you silly girl! Gunnar is planning on using your fortunes to save his family's business."

What is she talking about? Lana wondered. After their first encounter with Gunnar, she had looked him up online and discovered that his family owned hundreds of retail locations across America, Canada, and Europe. They had just opened ten more locations in Oregon, alone. If the groom's family owned one of the most successful sporting goods companies in the world, why would his family push him to marry for money?

Audrey looked at the woman as if she was a piece of dirt on her shoe. "Now you're making up lies about his family? What is wrong with you, Maureen?"

Lana and Willow exchanged glances. "Aha! So this is the infamous aunt Maureen."

"She's certainly no pushover," Lana whispered back.

Maureen continued lecturing her niece in a tone Lana would have used in a business meeting. There was no love or warmth in her voice or actions. "Their sporting goods stores are not as financially sound as they claim. Our accountant did a little digging and discovered that they've overextended themselves and the banks are about to call in several of their loans."

"You asked our family's accountant to investigate my fiancé? What is wrong with you?" Audrey screeched.

"The news should be hitting the papers in a few days. If you won't cancel the wedding, will you at least delay it? You shouldn't enter into marriage under false pretenses," Maureen reasoned.

A wave of confusion momentarily washed away Audrey's smug expression. "I don't believe you. And even if that were true, it's too late. I already changed my will. Gunnar is now the main beneficiary of my trust fund—not you."

"What!" Audrey's aunt stumbled backwards with her hand on her heart, as if her niece had shot her. "But why? You aren't even married yet."

"Because we are leaving for our honeymoon right after the wedding and I didn't want to have to deal with all the paperwork before we flew out," Audrey explained.

"Gunnar doesn't know you changed your will yet, does he?"

"Of course he does. I trust him far more than I do you, Maureen."

"You have always been so naïve. You can't take everyone's word at face value, you stupid girl. He doesn't love you—he's just after your money!"

Audrey's slap reverberated across the lobby.

"And you are a delusional old spinster who doesn't want to lose her golden goose. I am not a child anymore, and I was never yours to begin with."

"After all I did for you! How dare you—"

"Tell the truth?" Audrey leaned in close. "You were never there for me. All you did was hire others to care for me. But they were the help, not family. You have never been a mother to me! All you're worried about is losing your allowance."

Her aunt pulled herself up and began to retort when Audrey held up her hand, stopping Maureen from speaking. "After we get back from our honeymoon, my husband and I are going to live in my house, and I don't want you interfering in our lives. You are no longer welcome there. I want you out before we return."

Her aunt's tone finally was infused with emotion, in this case desperation, as she pleaded with her niece. "You promised I would always have a home there. It's certainly large enough—we could live in separate wings and never see each other."

"I don't care. You have mooched off of me long enough—it's time you get a life and let me live mine," Audrey retorted. "Be certain your things are out of my house before we get back."

When her aunt began to protest, Audrey began wailing so loudly that her bridesmaids circled around her.

"Can't you just leave Audrey alone?" Bianca cried. "She's been through so much today."

"She obviously doesn't want you here," Tabitha added.

When the hotel's security staff began to walk towards her, Maureen raised a fist in the air. "You haven't heard the last of me yet! Don't let Gunnar trick you out of your parents' money."

"Get out!" Audrey wailed.

"If you ignore me, you will regret it, Audrey. Mark my words," Maureen declared, before stalking out of the lobby.

16

Puffin for Dinner

When Lana and Willow entered the hotel's dining area, neither woman thought the bachelorette party would be present, let alone jovial. After that public showdown with Aunt Maureen, Lana figured they would have been in the bar, drinking the night away.

Yet, there they were, filling the largest table, a round of drinks already on it.

"Why does this keep happening?" Willow asked as she nodded at the only free table for two, smack dab next to the group. "Should we skip the puffin?"

"We can't seem to get away from those women, can we? Let's not allow them to spoil our night. I know puffins are adorable, but I do kind of want to try it," Lana admitted.

"Alright, then let's do this." Willow led the way to the table, doing her best to keep her back to the fivesome as she took her seat. Lana did the same. She picked up the menu, a single sheet with only a few lines of text, and attempted to read it. The dining room was quite dimly lit, thanks to the preference for candle lighting. Before she could decipher the selection, a waitress was already at her elbow.

"Welcome! Tonight's meal is a special one. To start, we have a selection of Icelandic appetizers that I am certain you will enjoy. Afterwards, it is time to try roasted puffin in a lovely berry sauce. Many tourists say it is the best meal they've had in Iceland." The young woman blushed as she spoke, making Lana wonder about the truth of the statement.

"Would you care for an aperitif?"

"I'd love a red wine. How about you, Lana?"

"That sounds divine," she sighed in happiness. Thanks to their long hikes and the extra drama this morning, Lana was pretty worn out and happy to simply relax and enjoy the evening.

The glasses of red wine were quickly followed by three small platters of appetizers.

"Here we have hákarl, or fermented shark meat." The waitress pointed to a plate full of fleshy cubes served on long toothpicks. "Because it has a high ammoniac content, we advise you to pinch your nose when taking the first bite."

"That's what I smell—I thought someone had just cleaned the table," Willow said.

"It is worth trying. And Iceland is one of the few places you can order it," the waitress said, a touch of pride in her voice, before pointing to the next dish. "This is hangikjöt, or smoked lamb. It combines well with the rye bread. And last, we have harðfiskur, or dried fish. It is one of the most popular foods in Iceland. Enjoy!"

She smiled briefly before darting back towards the kitchen.

Willow licked her lips. "My, oh my, this all looks quite interesting."

"I do like trying new foods," Lana agreed. She placed a thin slice of lamb onto a thick slab of rye bread and took a bite. "Delicious. The meat is really nice. A little smoky and salty, but you can still taste the lamb."

Willow picked up a toothpick of shark. "Here goes nothing." She pinched her nose and popped the cube into her mouth, chewing rapidly. The pained expression on her face said enough before she even swallowed.

"You do have to try it, but it's not for me," Willow said. She popped a thin piece of fried fish into her mouth. "Yum, that's more like it. The butter makes it taste sweeter than I'd expected."

Lana also pinched her nose and swallowed a cube of shark meat. The fermentation process made it chewier than she'd expected. "It's not horrible, but it is an acquired taste. I think I'll skip the shark. But I do love the rest."

After bringing drinks and food to Lana's table, their waitress had served the bachelorette party the same platters of appetizers. Apparently the younger women had already had a few drinks before they arrived, because all were a bit tipsy—especially the bride-to-be. They sampled the food, loudly critiquing it as they ate. Between bites, they took selfies and group shots, documenting most of their evening's meal.

That accounted for their obsession with their makeup, Lana figured, noting that the younger women seemed to reapply their lipstick, blush, or mascara after almost every bite. To Lana, they were taking the idea of being Instagram-ready to the max. Couldn't a Generation Z'er just enjoy a meal, without having to worry about being caught off-guard on camera?

Before Lana and Willow could finish their appetizers, the kitchen doors opened and a team of waiters brought out more trays of food. The head waiter announced, "Tonight's special, smoked puffin with blueberry Brennivín sauce. We hope you enjoy it!"

After their dinner was served, Lana looked down at the little lump of roasted meat on her plate, an equal-sized lump forming in her throat. One glance at her friend told her that she wasn't alone in feeling odd.

Willow whispered, "This is a weird choice, considering we are going to see them tomorrow."

The bachelorettes also seemed to question their choice of meal, however, for other reasons. Audrey in particular seemed to have trouble with the main dish. "Is it red meat? I have to fit into that dress or Gunnar will kill me. I don't want to embarrass him in front of his family. I know he would say a salad is better."

Destiny rolled her eyes. "Live a little, Audrey! A few bites of meat won't kill you. And Iceland is the only place in the world where you can eat puffin."

"If anything, you've lost weight this week. I'm certain you are going to look fabulous," Bianca added.

"Besides, they say puffin tastes like fish. And fish is good for you, right?" Tabitha chimed in.

Lana took a tentative bite, pleasantly surprised by the meaty texture and fishy taste. The berries in the sauce reminded her of slightly bitter cranberries and complemented the smoky flavor of the bird.

Willow nodded in approval. "It's pretty good. It reminds me of a slightly overcooked cod filet."

"I am curious to try it," Bianca said before taking a big bite of the dark-colored meat.

Audrey took a tiny bite, a grimace on her face as she let the meat slide onto her tongue.

"Oh, it's so bitter!" She took a big swig of her drink, as if to clean her mouth of the puffin's strong flavors. "Somehow it's making me feel light-headed, as well. Yuck."

"Mine's kind of bitter, too. I think it's those berries." Destiny's nose crinkled.

Audrey poked at her dish and moved its contents around, grimacing as she did. "Sorry, but this is not my kind of meal. Maybe they can make me a salad. I want to ask them to turn the heater down, anyway. It's stuffy in here!"

Lana looked to Willow, who appeared to be just as confused. "Do you think it's stuffy?" she whispered. "I'm still shivering underneath all of these layers. If anything, they can turn the heater up."

"Before I forget again, I want to thank you all for coming over to Iceland this week." Audrey stood up and raised her glass, partially filled with a fruity concoction that looked to be a frozen raspberry daiquiri. "To me and Gunnar, and all of you lovelies for being here to help us celebrate our new life together!"

"To Audrey and Gunnar," the three blondes squealed. Elaine also raised her glass, albeit less enthusiastically than the rest.

"What gives, Elaine? You've been acting even more depressed than usual tonight," Audrey said, the irritation in her voice evident.

"I don't mean to be a party pooper, but what if your aunt is right and Gunnar's family is pushing him into marrying you? He's so controlling, he could be lying to you and you wouldn't know it. Maybe you should talk to your accountants and lawyers before you two tie the knot on Friday? You deserve someone who treats you like a queen—I would hate for him to take advantage of you."

Audrey slammed her drink down onto the table. *"Et tu,* Elaine? I'm so tired of all of this drama! I don't want you at my wedding, after all."

Elaine shot up, almost tipping the table with her knees. Tabitha and Destiny grabbed the edges, keeping the drinks and food from spilling off of it.

"You know what, I don't want to go to your wedding anyway. And *Vogue* was wrong—there is no perfect number of bridesmaids. The only requirement is that they are your friends. Too bad you don't seem to have any real ones."

"That's it—get out of here! I don't want to see you anymore!" Audrey screeched as she pointed towards the door.

Elaine strode off, tears already streaming down her face, despite her bravado.

"Wait, Elaine! Audrey didn't mean it—" Bianca called out as she quickly rose and threw up an arm, as if to wave Elaine back.

"Who cares about Elaine! What about me?" Audrey cried out, shifting the attention back onto her. Her bottom lip pushed out as tears sprung from her eyes.

Tabitha, Destiny, and Bianca leaned over the table to pat her hand and squeeze her shoulder.

"There, there. I always said that Elaine wasn't one of us. She just doesn't care about the same things we do," Tabitha soothed.

"And you are always so nice to her! Too nice, if you ask me. She had no business telling you what to do. Gunnar is the catch of a lifetime. You'd be a fool not to marry him," Bianca cooed. She raised up her drink, encouraging the others to do the same.

"To Audrey and Gunnar!"

As their daiquiris met in the air, Lana felt a chill run up her spine. It must be from their frozen concoctions, she figured, shivering again just thinking about drinking that icy beverage. It was summer here, but still hadn't hit fifty degrees since she'd arrived.

"What are we going to do about Elaine?" Destiny asked.

Audrey tossed back her hair. "I don't care what she does, but she's not welcome to spend another minute with us. I hope she's smart enough to stay away from the church on Friday because I might snap if she tries to weasel her way back into the wedding."

She picked up her cocktail glass and downed the last of the alcoholic slushie in one gulp. "Waiter! We need another round over here!" she demanded, her voice slightly slurred. When she spotted a waiter coming out of the kitchen, she half rose out of her chair and waved him over. However, when she tried to call out to him, she fell back into her chair, instead. As Lana watched, Audrey's eyes shot open wide and she grabbed at her throat.

"Audrey, are you alright?" Destiny cried, the concern in her voice evident.

Everyone in the dining room seemed to turn to see what the commotion was.

"Can't—breathe." Audrey choked out the words, still clutching her throat.

Lana called out, "Get her some orange juice—she's a diabetic and it sounds like she's going into shock!"

"Forget the juice. Somebody call an ambulance!" Destiny shrieked as Audrey's head fell back and her eyelids drooped closed.

"Audrey, stay with us!" Bianca shoved her way in between Destiny and Audrey, shaking Audrey's shoulders as she tried rousing her friend out of unconsciousness.

"Stop, you're hurting her!" Tabitha cried and grabbed Bianca's hands.

"So woozy," Audrey gasped. Her eyes bulged open again, and she clawed at her throat, as if something was wrapped around it. Sweat poured from her skin as she swayed in her chair. Seconds later, her eyes rolled to the back of her head.

"Audrey! Can you hear me?" Bianca cried.

Audrey's head wobbled as she tried to crane her neck up. But the movement proved too much. Instead, her body went limp and she slipped down into the chair.

"Someone has to do something—she's dying!" Tabitha cried, tears pouring from her eyes.

Bianca pointed to Lana and shrieked, "You know CPR—help her!"

Lana sprung up. She had hoped someone in the room was a doctor or nurse, but no one offered their help. And since no one else volunteered, Lana felt obligated to try to save Audrey. "We need to get her onto the floor."

The bridesmaids gently moved their friend out of the chair and onto the floor. The other diners were silent as they watched the scene unfold.

Lana leaned over Audrey, noting her raspy breath. She gently tilted up her chin and was about to begin mouth-to-mouth resuscitation, when a trail of foam dribbled from Audrey's lips.

Lana sprung back. "This can't be happening again!"

"Why aren't you doing anything? Help her already!" Bianca screamed.

Lana sat on the floor, frozen in the knowledge that Audrey was not having a diabetic reaction. This seemed more like poison.

"Someone has to help her!" Tabitha screeched.

When a waiter attempted to shove Lana aside so as to begin CPR, she shoved him back, only harder.

"Don't touch her! There's foam coming out of her mouth. That's not right. If she's been poisoned, whoever puts their mouth onto hers might get sick, as well."

The young waiter also jumped back, putting distance between himself and Audrey.

"This is absurd!" Bianca pushed them both aside and bent over the bride-to-be, whose eyes were glazed over and lips were now turning blue. "You're letting my friend die! Tell me what to do."

Before Bianca could bend down, more foam began bubbling out of Audrey's mouth. The waiter pulled her away from her friend. "I think that lady's right, we shouldn't touch her."

The bridesmaids gathered around their friend, crying as they watched Audrey slowly slip away. As Audrey drew her final breath, the three blondes burst into tears and fell into each other's arms.

Lana choked up as well, horrified that another person had died in her presence. Audrey was young, wealthy, and about to marry the man of her dreams. Yet someone stole her life, instead. In Lana's mind, the foam indicated poison, which meant someone in this room was a murderer.

As the realization set in, Lana's shoulders slumped. *Not again.*

17

Consumed by Grief

The minutes after Audrey's death were pure chaos. The waitstaff rushed around the room, seemingly unable to sit still but also unsure as to what they were supposed to do, until the manager burst into the dining room. "The police are on their way. Please follow me to the lobby—this is now a potential crime scene."

After the diners and staff were ushered into the hotel lobby, a security guard was stationed in front of the closed doors to the dining hall, effectively sealing it off until the police arrived.

Tabitha, Bianca, and Destiny sat on one couch, their arms wrapped around each other as they grieved the loss of their friend.

"I can't believe she's gone," Tabitha wailed.

"This isn't fair. Audrey was far too young. She had her whole life ahead of her," Bianca cried.

Lana couldn't keep her eyes off of the dining room doors.

"Lana, I know what you are thinking, but you are not an angel of death," Willow insisted.

She nodded, though her heart remained heavy. "That poor girl. She was far too young to die. And she was about to be married."

"To a rather arrogant young man who flirts with anything that moves. I don't know if it would have been a lengthy union," Willow reasoned.

"It doesn't matter," Lana snapped. "It's just...another person died while on tour with me. It's messing with my head."

Willow threw an arm around her shoulders. "There has to be a reason why this keeps happening. Hopefully we can figure it out together."

As much as Lana wanted to get away, she and Willow hovered around the lobby with the rest. Technically, they had nothing to do with the bachelorette party or Audrey's death, but experience told her that the police would want to interview everyone who was present in the dining room. So they milled about, until Bianca sprung up and rushed over to them.

"Why would you say that she was poisoned? It must have been her diabetes. She has been having trouble with her insulin since we arrived," Bianca insisted before turning to address the entire lobby.

"It is because of you that Audrey is dead. If you had let us start the CPR right away, we might have saved her. I'm going to tell the police about you interfering as soon as they get here!"

Lana felt like Bianca had punched her in the gut. "I was trying to protect the rest of you, in case she was poisoned. You're right—I'm no doctor so I cannot be certain. Unfortunately, I've had to deal with this sort of thing on my tours and it sure seemed like her body reacted rapidly and badly to something. The foam coming out of her mouth and her blue lips seemed to indicate that she was poisoned."

"Wait—you've had poisoners in your tour groups? What company do you work for? I want to be sure to avoid it," Bianca quipped.

"How could Audrey have been poisoned? We all shared the appetizers. If there was something in them, why don't any of us feel sick?" Destiny said.

"Did you share the puffin, too?"

"No, we all had our own servings."

"If there was something in her meal, it must have been fast-acting because she'd only taken a few bites of it," Bianca said. "And if her puffin was poisoned, then anyone working in the kitchen could have done it. I bet you money one of Gunnar's ex-girlfriends did this."

Bianca looked pointedly over at the waitresses and cooks gathered on one side of the lobby. "Gunnar liked to brag that he left a trail of broken hearts in Iceland when Audrey agreed to marry him."

"The police should be able to test all of the dishes and see if there was anything suspicious in any of them," Lana said, keeping her voice as calm as possible.

When the sirens wailing in the distance grew increasingly louder, Destiny pulled her phone out of her tiny purse. "Someone has to tell Gunnar. I'll do it."

Bianca snatched the phone out of Destiny's hands. "I should do it. I've known him much longer than you have."

"How's that? Audrey's the one who introduced you to him, remember?" Destiny grabbed her phone back. "We used to date, he would expect me to call."

Lana couldn't believe how they were reacting. Their good friend lay dead a few feet away, yet they seemed more interested in calling the groom than mourning their friend.

The click of high heels rapidly approaching made Lana turn.

"What is wrong with you?" Audrey's aunt raged, echoing her thoughts. "My darling niece is lying there dead, and you two are fighting about who gets to tell her fiancé the news? I warned her about her supposed friends trying to seduce her boyfriend. And now it doesn't matter if I'm right or not. My poor Audrey."

The aunt broke into tears, covering her face with her hands as her body shook.

Bianca gaped at the older woman. "What are you doing here? I thought Audrey told you to leave."

"I flew over here to make certain she and Gunnar didn't marry and I wasn't going to leave until I had done so. That seems so trivial now! Oh, Audrey. I've let your father down." Maureen began weeping openly as she stared at the closed dining room doors.

"Did she suffer?" the aunt asked through her tears.

Destiny patted her arm. "No, I don't think so. She felt a little woozy before she passed out. And then she was gone."

The meant-to-be-comforting news only brought more tears to the aunt's eyes.

"Oh, my darling niece!" As her wails intensified, one of the receptionists came over and wrapped an arm around her.

Lana was grateful that someone else had taken the initiative. She wanted to be an onlooker, for once, instead of an active participant in this murder investigation.

18

Accident or Murder

Flashing lights signaled the arrival of the ambulance and police. When a team of paramedics rushed inside, the security guard opened the dining room door for them and pointed to Audrey's corpse, still lying on the floor next to her table.

Following close behind were six uniformed police officers and an older, more formally dressed man Lana assumed to be a detective. His severe expression and beady eyes made her cringe. The manager raced over to the detective and began babbling in Icelandic. After pointing to the kitchen staff, waiters, and diners present at the time of the death, now spread out across the vast lobby, he stepped back and let the police take over.

Before the senior officer could make a move, Maureen rushed towards the detective so quickly, Lana thought she was going to hug him. "Oh good, you're finally here. My poor niece is dead and I know who did it—it was Gunnar Jónsson!"

The detective froze midstep, then turned to Audrey's aunt. "Gunnar Jónsson, as in the son of Jón Gunnarsson, owner of John's Sporting Goods?"

"One and the same," Maureen said, with disdain in her voice.

The detective seemed to stand up a little straighter, and his tone grew even more formal. "How is he involved?"

"Gunnar and Audrey were set to marry on Friday."

Lana swore the senior officer's already pale face drained completely of color.

"Gunnar's family must be a big deal around here. Did you see how that detective reacted?" Willow whispered.

Lana nodded in agreement.

"But Gunnar wasn't even here," Bianca exclaimed. "How could he have killed Audrey?"

Maureen pointed an accusatory finger at the three bridesmaids. "One of you must have helped him kill her. Which one of you was it? I know you all worship him; pretty much every young thing that he comes into contact with him does."

"Why do you suspect Gunnar?" the detective asked in a quiet voice.

"Because he tricked Audrey into making him her sole heir. And now she's dead, and he's a billionaire! What more motive do you need? I always knew this would happen, that someone would take advantage of her because of her wealth. I just didn't expect it to be someone from such an upstanding family."

While Tabitha and Destiny cowered under Maureen's gaze, Bianca appeared defiant.

"That's funny. A few hours ago, Audrey kicked you out of her house after telling you that she'd disinherited you. I bet you killed her out of spite," Bianca said. "And now you're blaming Gunnar and us to divert the police from the truth—that you did this!"

"How dare you accuse me of harming my precious niece! I gave up my life to raise her—why would I wait until now to kill her?"

"You hated Audrey! You probably figured if you killed her before she married Gunnar, that you would inherit everything. But you're wrong about that," Bianca taunted.

"Why you little—"

When the aunt lunged at the bridesmaid, a police officer sprung in between the two women.

Bianca turned to the senior officer. "After Audrey told her to leave, Maureen could have snuck into the kitchen and put something into her food."

The detective cocked his head. "Wouldn't someone working in the kitchen have noticed? And how would she have known which plate would be served to Audrey?"

"Maybe she put poison in all of the dishes, but only Audrey was susceptible because of her diabetes," Bianca suggested. "If Maureen didn't do it, one of the waitstaff could have killed her that way. I bet one of them used to date Gunnar—he really got around from what Audrey told me. They could have killed her out of jealousy."

"Interesting theory," the detective said, though his tone made clear that he did not agree with Bianca's presumptions. He then turned his gaze towards the rest. "When the manager called this in, he mentioned that someone suspected she'd been poisoned."

"It was that tour guide," Tabitha replied.

"It's her fault that Audrey's dead!" Bianca cried as she pointed to Lana. "She refused to let anyone perform CPR."

"Miss?" The detective turned to Lana. "Would you care to explain?"

"Great, so much for staying out of it," she mumbled to Willow before raising her voice. "Audrey seemed to become unwell while she was eating the puffin. She had already mentioned that she felt warm before she had trouble breathing. And after she passed out, foam started coming out of her mouth and her lips began to turn blue. She reacted so suddenly, I just assumed that someone had poisoned her meal. It was instinct, but I have no proof," was all Lana could manage. If the police officer found out she had been involved with multiple murder investigations, she might be here all night.

The detective nodded once before elevating his voice. "Before we continue, let me examine the body and talk to the paramedics. Everyone is to remain in the lobby."

He hustled towards the dining room before anyone could try to delay him further.

The bachelorettes took positions on a couch across from Willow and Lana, before engaging the pair in a staring contest. Lana could only shake her head and look away; she had no desire to play these childish games.

Willow put a hand over her mouth and whispered to Lana, "This is ridiculous! We were only trying to help, and now they are trying to pin Audrey's death on you."

Lana smirked in response.

When the detective returned several minutes later, his expression was even more somber than when he arrived.

As soon as the door opened, Bianca sprung up. "Was it poison?"

He and two of his officers approached the bridesmaids.

"We will have to wait for the medical reports, but the physical evidence does indicate a fatal reaction to either a medicine or a poison, which means I will be treating this as a suspicious death, until we know more."

He turned to Lana. "That was a smart move, keeping the others away from the body."

Willow's hip bumped her, but Lana felt no satisfaction. A woman was dead, most likely murdered, at the table next to hers. And they were both members of the same tour group, to boot. "This is doing my head in, Willow. Dotty might be right after all."

Willow grabbed her hand and squeezed tight. "Nonsense. Put that thought right out of your mind."

"Before we discuss this evening further, let us take a step back. Who are you and how are you connected to our victim?"

"We are Audrey's best friends. We all flew over together for her bachelorette party," Bianca stated, taking control of the conversation. Destiny and Tabitha seemed happy to let her do so.

"I'm her maid of honor," Bianca said with pride, before hesitatingly adding, "Or I was supposed to be."

"When did you arrive in Reykjavik, and when did this bachelorette party take place?"

"Last Saturday," Bianca replied. "She and Gunnar were to be married Friday morning. Audrey wanted to make a week of it and really let loose before they tied the knot." The young woman wiped away a tear and looked to the ground.

"And all four of you flew over together from the United States?"

"Yes, from Portland, Oregon. Oh! Elaine flew over with us, as well. But she left the dinner just before Audrey collapsed," Tabitha said.

"And where is Elaine now?"

"I don't know—her room, I guess. She and Audrey got into a big fight and Elaine stormed off, but we all stayed."

"And what was this fight about?"

"It was more of a disagreement, really," Destiny said. "Elaine was only trying to be a friend, but her timing was off."

When the detective raised his brow, Bianca took over again. "What Destiny is trying to say is that Elaine thought Audrey and Gunnar were rushing into this marriage. But two days before the wedding isn't really the best time to bring it up, is it? Especially from one of the bridesmaids. If I was Audrey, I would have done the same thing."

The detective nodded, encouraging Bianca to continue. When no explanation came, he asked, "And what exactly did Audrey do?"

"She uninvited Elaine to her wedding."

"Do you mean she told one of her bridesmaids not to come to her wedding?" The detective had trouble keeping the incredulity out of his voice. "That must have been some argument."

"Yes, that's exactly what I'm saying. Their disagreement was quite loud. I'm sure everyone else heard it too. Right?" Bianca looked over to Lana and Willow, who both nodded.

"She's right, they were practically screaming at each other," Willow confirmed.

"And you two are also here for the wedding?" the detective asked Lana and Willow.

"No, we aren't. I arrived last week," Lana replied, unsure how to explain her reason for being in Iceland.

"And I flew in from Seattle on Sunday because I couldn't get away from work any earlier. We're here on vacation," Willow replied. "We'd never met Audrey or her friends before arriving in Reykjavik."

"Didn't Audrey also fire Elaine?" Bianca said, drawing the detective's attention back to the bachelorettes.

"So Elaine was an employee and a friend of the deceased?" the detective clarified.

"Yes, she's one of Audrey's gardeners, and they'd gotten to know each other pretty well over the years," Destiny confirmed.

"Alright, why don't we ask Elaine to come down to the lobby." The detective nodded to one of the officers standing next to him, who walked over to the reception desk.

"You say the deceased had diabetes, but she was not wearing a medical bracelet," the officer asked.

"Stop saying that. Her name is Audrey, and she hates those bracelets," Destiny growled, clearly unable to use the past tense. "She might have kept one in her toiletry bag, in case the airline questioned her medicine supply. But I can't be certain."

"We'll have an officer check Audrey's room," the detective said in a gentler tone. He signaled to another officer to go look for it.

"What if she overdosed on insulin? Are you going to conduct a toxicology report?" Bianca asked. "She's been having trouble with her diabetes all week."

"This isn't like in television shows where it takes a few minutes to get a clear result. A toxicology report takes weeks," he said wearily. Lana could imagine how television and films had changed the way people thought of his work. "But a preliminary toxicology report, a standard test in this kind of situation, can shed some light on what may have killed her."

He pulled out a notebook. "What else can you tell me about this evening? Did the deceased, I mean Audrey, feel unwell before you entered the dining room? Had she ever mentioned receiving threatening letters or having a stalker?"

Tabitha shook her head resolutely. "No, nothing like that. She had been feeling poorly all week, but we all assumed it was because of the jet leg and stress of her upcoming wedding. But it was really obvious that she was enjoying herself, and that she couldn't wait to get married to Gunnar."

An officer approached the detective, a metal bracelet in his hand. The two exchanged words before the senior officer turned back to the Americans.

"According to the medical bracelet found in Audrey's toiletry bag, your friend was a diabetic and also allergic to penicillin. Did you all know about both ailments?"

Destiny shook her head. "Only about the diabetes because she had to inject herself with insulin pretty regularly. But Audrey never talked openly about her illness. She tried to ignore it as much as possible and live a normal life."

The detective glanced over at Tabitha and Bianca.

"I had no idea," Tabitha emphasized as Bianca nodded in agreement.

"Alright. For now, I am going to ask you to remain at the hotel. My medical team will need some time to work out the cause of death. After they do, we may need to speak with you again."

"Wait—are we suspects in our friend's murder?" Bianca spat the words at the officer.

"No, but you knew her best, and considering we are thousands of miles from her home, I may need to find out more about her medical background and family history. Do you understand?"

Bianca nodded tersely.

"Good. One of my officers will take down your contact information, then you are free to leave the hotel lobby. Thank you for your cooperation," he said before looking over to the dining room staff, sitting in the other corner of the lobby.

He had begun to cross over to them, when one of his officers and Elaine stepped out of the elevator. The detective veered towards them instead and pulled Elaine aside. After a brief conversation with the last bridesmaid, he approached the restaurant workers.

After the detective left her, Elaine glanced over in the direction of the remaining bachelorettes, still huddled together on the couch, but didn't walk over. Instead, she made a point of turning on her heel and heading to the hotel bar.

"There is something strange about that one," Bianca said.

"I still don't get why Audrey asked her to be one of her bridesmaids. She never really had anything nice to say about Elaine," Tabitha chimed in.

"All that money and privilege, and yet no real friends," Willow whispered to Lana.

Lana's heart saddened at the thought. "I am so lucky to have you and Dotty in my life."

19

First Arrest

After they allowed a junior officer to record their names and passport numbers, Willow turned to Lana.

"What a night! Do you want to go back up to the room or should we have a drink first?"

Lana looked to the bar where Elaine was parked on a tall stool, her hand wrapped around a fruity concoction. "I am too wound up to sleep. I think a drink is in order."

When Willow turned and spotted Elaine, a wicked smile crossed her face. "Are you really keyed up, or do you want to do a little investigating?"

"Maybe Elaine knows what happened to Audrey. I mean, we didn't see and hear everything. As much as it looked like she'd been poisoned, I do hope it was an accidental overdose or a fatal combination of medicines. It would be nice to know that it wasn't murder this time."

They approached the younger woman, who was clearly down in the dumps. Elaine seemed to be the only bridesmaid affected by Audrey's death, Lana realized. The other three appeared to be more concerned with Gunnar than his now-deceased bride.

Elaine looked up at the pair, a miserable expression on her face. "I know Audrey was not the smartest or kindest person on the planet, but she didn't deserve to die like that. Who could have done this to her?"

"Maybe nobody did. Audrey had so many medical issues; perhaps her body reacted badly to the combination of alcohol and food somehow. You hear about that sometimes, young celebrities drinking too much after popping a few pills, and then they have a heart attack or slip into a coma and never wake up," Lana thought aloud, grasping at straws.

"Maybe," Elaine sniffed. "That would be better than if someone had intentionally killed her. But it still won't bring Audrey back."

When Elaine broke out into tears, Lana hesitated before patting her lightly on the back. "If someone did hurt her intentionally, I'm sure the police will figure it out and arrest them. Gunnar's family is famous here; that's sure to help."

The bartender approached them, interrupting the conversation as he nodded to Lana and Willow. "What can I get you?"

"Two mint teas with honey, please," Lana said.

"Are you sure? I was thinking something a little stronger." Willow turned to the bartender. "What would you recommend as a nightcap?"

Before the man could suggest something, a commotion in the lobby attracted their attention.

"This is absurd!"

Maureen's indignation was apparent, even from the bar.

"You may think so, but I still require your assistance," said the detective patiently. "Help me get into your mind space—you just had a terrible fight with your precious niece, as you called her, during which she kicks you out of her house and disinherits you. And then, immediately afterwards, you go into the kitchen and make small talk with the cooks."

Maureen sighed heavily, making clear that this was a waste of time. "Audrey is a stubborn young woman, but she is the only family I have. It's been me and Audrey for almost twenty years, and then Gunnar sweeps her off her feet and all of sudden I am the bad guy!"

"That still doesn't explain your being in the kitchen."

"I love to cook, and it keeps my mind off of my troubles. After that nasty argument, I didn't want to be alone. But I didn't want to sit in the bar and drown my sorrows, either. So I retreated to my happy place, the kitchen. I'm sorry if it upset the staff, but they didn't seem bothered. In fact, the cooks were really generous in sharing their recipes with me. So much so that by the time I went up to my hotel room, I was in a much better mood. That is, until I heard the commotion in the lobby and discovered that my niece was dead."

She glared at the detective, as if it was his fault that Audrey had been harmed. "You have to interview Gunnar. He's behind this somehow, I just know he is. As soon as Audrey told me she'd changed her will, I knew her days were numbered. I just didn't expect him to act so quickly."

"We will certainly investigate every possible lead, but I do have one more question for you. Why did you ask which plates were meant for Audrey's table?"

"I don't know. Curiosity, I guess." For the first time, Maureen's voice wavered.

"And when they told you it was random who got which plate—why did you become upset and storm out of the kitchen?"

"Did I?" she replied, vaguely. "No, I'm certain I skipped out of there. The cooks and waiters were all so busy getting the dinners ready, they must have remembered it wrong."

The detective eyed her warily. "I would like to know more about your decision to visit Iceland and your relationship with your niece. Why don't we go back to the station and continue our conversation there?"

"No thank you. My niece is dead; I would like to have a margarita and think about her wasted life."

"It wasn't a request," the detective said softly.

"Are you arresting me?"

"No, but if you do not come and talk with us willingly, we will be forced to take you into custody."

When two uniformed officers approached her on either side, Maureen looked around the lobby wildly. "I didn't do this—Gunnar did! I feel it in my bones! Don't let him get away with this!"

"Ma'am, if you refuse to come with us, then I have no choice but to arrest you."

"Alright already, just keep your hands off of my Armani jacket. It's worth more than you make in a month."

Elaine rolled her eyes. "She's so stuck up, even the police are beneath her."

After the officers wrangled Maureen out of the hotel, Lana asked, "Do you think she could have hurt Audrey?"

"I don't think so. But I don't know who else would have. I guess one of the blondes could have done it, but why? Gunnar wasn't going to choose one of them over Audrey. She was the richest one of the bunch, and money is what he seemed to love most. Well, and himself."

"And now that Audrey is, um, out of the picture?" Lana gently pressed.

Elaine's eyes widened as Lana's implication sunk in. A moment later, she twisted her neck and eyed the three blondes warily.

"Tabitha is the one I would watch out for. That girl worships money perhaps even more than Gunnar. Now that he is Audrey's beneficiary, I can imagine he's worth quite a lot. Even if what Audrey's aunt said about his family being bankrupt is true, he won't have to worry about money ever again. And Tabitha knows it."

"What about Bianca? Is she as obsessed with wealth, do you think?"

"I can't do this." Elaine sprung off her chair. "It's just too much to take in. Audrey's dead and you think one of her friends may have done it? I need to be alone. Please excuse me." The young woman fled the bar before Lana or Willow could respond.

"Wow, Audrey's death really affected her. It's too bad her friends aren't as empathetic." Willow nodded at the three remaining bridesmaids. As she did, the dining room doors opened and Audrey's body was brought out on a stretcher.

The three blonde bridesmaids grew quiet when she was wheeled past. "Should we go with her?" Destiny asked.

Bianca shivered. "I would rather not take a trip to the morgue."

"But we are her friends. I hate leaving her alone like that," Tabitha said.

"Maybe they aren't as heartless as we thought," Willow whispered.

"Has anyone heard back from Gunnar?" Destiny asked. "He really needs to know what has happened."

"Let me check." Bianca grabbed her phone and unlocked the screen. Her disappointed expression made clear he had not.

"Oh, well. I guess we'll have to keep trying."

20

Early Morning Surprise

Thursday—Day Three of the Southern Island Tour of Iceland

A loud knock on the neighboring door woke Lana from a restless slumber. Audrey's death had hit her hard, and sleep was long in coming. Even though she didn't know the young woman or her friends, the fact that another person had died in her presence—and during an organized tour, no less—was unsettling and unnerving.

"Yes, who is it?" she heard Elaine call out. "Oh, give me a moment."

Her reaction made Lana rise to see who was knocking on Elaine's door. She could just make out an Icelandic police uniform, but she couldn't see who was wearing it. Only when the man spoke did she know for certain that it was the same detective who had interviewed them last night.

"Elaine Dumfries, I have a warrant to search your room and possessions. If you would please wait in the hallway, my officer will stay with you until we are finished."

"If you want to search through my stuff, all you had to do was ask. I have nothing to hide." Elaine's tone had switched from humble to irritated in a heartbeat.

"Good," Lana heard the detective say before the sound of footsteps and a door closing made its way to her.

Lana ran to Willow, still deep in sleep, and gently shook her shoulder.

When she reacted groggily, Lana whispered, "The police are in Elaine's room!"

"What?" Willow sprung out of bed and raced to the peephole.

When Lana realized that they couldn't share the view, she cracked the door open as softly as she could and crouched down so that Willow could still see, before putting one eye to the thin opening. From her position, she could see several other eyeballs staring through opened doors, clearly watching the drama unfolding in the hallway.

Elaine, for her part, remained calm as she waited out in the hallway for the detective to finish up.

Several minutes later, he emerged from her room, holding up Elaine's purse and a vial of medicine. "I noticed this prescription bottle in your purse last night, when you opened it to retrieve your passport. Are these your penicillin pills?"

"Yes, of course they are. My name is right on the bottle."

"Why are you taking penicillin?"

"Because I contracted Legionnaire's disease at work. I only have to take it for a few more days, at least, if the doctor gives me the all-clear at my next checkup."

"Alright, I see that this is a new bottle, issued only a week ago, and should contain forty pills."

Elaine shrugged. "It's what the doctor ordered."

"Then why are there only five pills remaining?"

Elaine's face twisted into a mask of shock. "No, there should be thirty-three in there. I only take one a day. It was practically full yesterday morning!"

"So you are saying that you do not know where the other pills are?"

"No! I mean, yes, that's what I'm saying. I don't know where they are or who would have taken them. But that bottle was full yesterday. If one of your officers didn't mess with it, then someone else did!"

"I am afraid I am going to have to ask you to come back to the station for further questioning."

"But why? I didn't harm Audrey. I wasn't even there when she died."

"Yes, but you were there when they served the drinks and puffin. And according to the preliminary reports, Audrey died from a severe allergic reaction to penicillin. Our lab is still testing the food and drinks on your table for traces of it. Several witnesses have mentioned that you and Audrey argued about your job just before her death, and she told you not to come to her wedding. Add in the missing medicine and I think we have plenty to talk about."

"Are you arresting me?" Elaine sputtered.

"Not yet. I'm only taking you in for questioning, at this time." The detective's tone remained neutral.

Elaine nodded once, then waved at her pajamas and hotel bathrobe. "Can I at least change my clothes?"

"Certainly. One of our female officers will accompany you."

Elaine turned towards her room, grumbling under her breath. The detective signaled for one of the female officers to stay with Elaine before turning to address the many guests peeking out from behind their hotel doors.

"The show is over. You can return to your rooms now," he said wryly before standing guard in front of Elaine's room.

"Did I hear him right—Elaine is being taken into custody?" Willow grabbed Lana's arm. 'That poor girl. Of that group, Elaine was the one I suspected the least."

"Me, too," Lana said with a frown.

"She seemed like the only normal one in the bunch. I can't imagine she killed Audrey so she could get to Gunnar, nor do I believe that she murdered her because she fired her. She didn't even want to be a gardener, remember? She wanted to open her own landscape design business."

"Which would never have gotten off the ground if Audrey had badmouthed Elaine to her wealthy friends."

"Okay, that would be problematic. But the other bridesmaids seem to have more reason to want Audrey out of the picture," Willow insisted.

"I see what you are doing, but I'm not interested in playing detective. This time, let's let the police do their jobs."

"Do you think they'll really investigate the three rich bridesmaids or snobby aunt, if they already have a viable suspect in custody?" Willow said, exasperated.

"Willow, can we please forget about the bachelorette party today? I just want to enjoy the puffin and whale watching tour. Is that too much to ask?"

Willow's expression softened. "I'll let it go for now. But we have all day to talk about Audrey's death."

Lana rolled her eyes as she crossed to the bathroom. "Can we at least get dressed and eat breakfast first? The bus leaves in an hour."

Before Willow could reply, she closed the door and turned on the shower, effectively ending the conversation.

21

Person of Interest

As much as Lana wanted to ignore Audrey's death and Elaine's arrest, it was all the hotel guests could talk about. Speculations about the murder method and killer's identity abounded as they walked through the packed breakfast hall towards the buffet. To Lana's chagrin, the only free table was close enough to the bridesmaids that they could hear their every word. Not that Lana had to strain her ears; Bianca, Tabitha, and Destiny were broadcasting their conversation around the room. Considering the general interest in Audrey's death and Elaine's arrest, Lana had to assume their louder-than-normal tone was intentional.

"Did you hear—Elaine has been arrested!" Lana overheard Bianca gleefully sharing this horrendous news with someone on the telephone. "Nah, they already released Maureen. I guess that means she didn't do it," Bianca said before pausing to listen. Seconds later she began to cackle with laughter. "I'll call you as soon as she's been charged with the crime," she promised before hanging up.

Great friends, Lana thought.

"Bianca, Elaine is not under arrest—I heard that hunk of a detective say that pretty clearly," Tabitha corrected. "But she is in custody. She's a, what do they call that again—a person with potential?"

"A person of interest," Bianca corrected.

Tabitha snapped her fingers. "Right. A person of interest. I bet that's just another way of saying that they are looking for a way to pin this crime on her."

"They won't have to look hard, if she really did it," Destiny pointed out. "Although she just doesn't seem the type to me. She was too into herself to really care what Audrey thought. And why would she want to harm her, anyway? I can't imagine Audrey had left anything to Elaine in her will. And Gunnar would never be interested in someone like her."

"Jealousy does make people do crazy things, and Audrey had everything Elaine did not," Tabitha stated, as if it was a fact.

"I bet she was madly in love with Gunnar, too," Bianca added. "But when she realized he would never fall for her, she pretended to hate him. And Audrey did fire her."

"But now that she's dead, Elaine is still out of a job. I can't imagine Audrey's aunt will be able to stay in the house, either. I bet it will be sold, unless Gunnar really does inherit all of Audrey's possessions. And I can't see Elaine wanting to work for him," Destiny said.

"Maybe Elaine did it, maybe she didn't. Either way, she did have the opportunity and motive, as the detective pointed out. But I wouldn't put it past a local to have done her in. The waiters and cooks could have poisoned the dish and made certain Audrey received it. Gunnar does have a way with women and does come back to Iceland every summer," Bianca said as she looked around the hall.

All of sudden, Bianca's voice rose an octave. "Say, Lana," the blonde bridesmaid asked, just as Lana took a bite of rye bread slathered with butter.

That's the first time she's gotten my name right, Lana thought as she responded by raising her eyebrows.

Bianca took it as a sign to come closer. "I'm sorry for pointing the finger at you last night," she said loudly. "My friend had just died, and I was upset and lashing out."

"It's okay, I understand," Lana said as diplomatically as possible, aware that all of the breakfast hall was following their conversation.

"Say, I heard you and your friend talking about how you'd solved a murder before. I don't trust the local police to get this right. So far they seem to be pointing the finger at everyone, and I wouldn't be surprised if they find a reason to blame the rest of us, as well. Even though we had nothing to do with our dear friend's death," Bianca exclaimed dramatically for their crowd. "Could you keep your eyes and ears open for us, just in case?"

Lana threw her hands up, as if to ward off Bianca's request. "I don't want to get involved."

"But you are involved," she said in a threatening tone that set Lana's nerves on edge. "We are all under suspicion until the police are certain they've caught the killer."

"She does have a point," Willow mumbled.

"You're just eager to play detective," Lana hissed under her breath.

Willow shrugged, but Lana saw the glint in her eye.

"Look, if I hear anything useful, I'll let you know, okay? All I'm asking for is a *quid pro quo*," Bianca said.

Didn't Hannibal Lector use that phrase often? Lana thought before shrugging. "Sure, okay. if I see or hear anything incriminating, I'll get in touch with you."

Bianca held out her hand. "It's a deal."

22

Guardian Angel

When the breakfast door opened, Bianca turned towards the noise, causing most of the diners to do the same. Standing in the threshold was Gunnar Jónsson, looking as attractive as ever, despite his slouched posture and wrinkled clothes.

"Oh, Gunnar! We've been trying to reach you!" Bianca ran towards him, but he sidestepped her embrace and fell into Destiny's arms, instead.

"I can't believe she's gone, Des. What do I do now? We were supposed to be getting married tomorrow." Gunnar buried his head in her shoulder and burst into tears.

"There, there. It's going to be alright," Destiny murmured into his hair as she rocked him back and forth.

"See, he does have a thing for Destiny," Lana murmured to Willow.

"And the rest do not like it. If looks could kill..." Willow nodded to the other two, who were glaring at Destiny.

"What is with them—do they all have a crush on Gunnar?"

"It sure seems like it. But he clearly favors one above the rest." Willow nodded to Destiny.

"That may be, but my watch tells me it's time to go to Puffin Island. I bet the bachelorettes won't be joining us for that trip."

"That's too bad, I would have liked to have studied their interactions more," Willow said.

"You are really getting into this sleuthing thing, aren't you?"

"It is addictive," Willow admitted.

Sure enough, when they boarded the bus that would whisk them off to their tour of Akurey Island, the surviving members of the bachelorette party were not on board. Soon, they were at the Old Harbor boarding a large boat with plenty of room on the outer decks for all of them, as well as a glassed-in deck that could seat fifty. Before they set sail, their guide explained the basic safety procedures and then advised them to take a seat for the short journey.

"Expect to see Atlantic puffins, Arctic terns, black guillemots, and northern fulmars. If we are lucky, dolphins may jump in our boat's wake. Akurey Island is known for its summertime colony of puffins. These funny little birds spend their winters in Ireland and Great Britain, and their summers here," their guide explained while he handed out the binoculars.

"I read in the brochure that we don't actually stop at the island, but only circle it. Why is that?" one guest asked.

"These islands are protected sanctuaries, so we are not allowed to land on them. But we actually have a better chance at seeing the birds from the boat, anyway. The puffins prefer to roost in the cliff faces and rocky outcrops, which you can't see from land. From our lower vantage point, the little birds' orange beaks contrast nicely with the gray cliffs and boulders."

Soon they were leaving the Old Harbor and maneuvering through several islands that seemed to protect the city from the ocean's stronger currents.

Once they had set sail, Willow and Lana headed outside. The winds swept salty spray into their eyes, but the sweeping views of the city center and surrounding mountains were worth it. On the horizon, they could see a storm moving in, and fast. By the time they arrived at Akurey Island, fifteen minutes later, the boat was rocking so much that Lana had trouble seeing through her binoculars.

However, once she got her sea legs, it became easier to focus on the jagged shoreline and rocky outcrops bobbing in front of them. The desolate islands were more like chunks of grass-covered stone with shorelines made up of boulders. But the rocky spaces were the perfect roosting places for puffins.

The little birds were almost invisible in amongst the rocks, until they turned and flashed their bright orange beaks. Soon, she and Willow were spotting dozens. While it was fun seeing them interact by their nesting sites, Lana loved how gracefully they dived into the water, more often than not with a fish in their colorful beaks when they surfaced.

Not all of the guests were having the same luck. Another standing on the other side of the boat exclaimed, "According to the brochure it sounded like they would be flying all around us! I haven't seen a single one."

"Keep searching," the guide encouraged. "They roost in the cliff faces and dive into the waters to find their food. If you keep your binoculars focused on the rocks, you should see several."

Lana agreed that they were more difficult to see than she had expected, but she still enjoyed trying and got a thrill each time she glimpsed one of them passing through the viewfinder of her binoculars.

A half hour in, the waves kicked up, and their boat began rocking so much that both she and Willow had trouble standing. They were not the only ones. Soon, a few of the older guests lost their balance and slipped out on the deck. After the third one went down hard on her hip, their guides ushered them back inside the glassed-in viewing area.

"If these waves get much worse, I might get seasick," Lana said.

"I know what you mean—I haven't felt this nauseated since I was pregnant with Zoe," Willow added.

They did their best to keep watching for signs of the little birds through the rain-spattered windows. But the waves were so choppy and the sky so gray, it was hard to tell the difference between a puffin and a blob of sea foam.

When one of the guides came to see whether they were doing alright, Lana couldn't help but ask about the weather conditions.

"The wind really has picked up, hasn't it?" the guide said cheerily. "Wait five minutes and it will probably change again!" She laughed before moving on to the next group.

Ten minutes later, when the weather had changed for the worst, the captain got on the loudspeaker and announced they would have to return to harbor and wait out the storm. A burst of lightning tore across the sky, as if to emphasis their worsening predicament.

"Well, we can't really see outside thanks to the rain, so we might as well finish our chat about Alex. I do fly back in a few days," Willow rushed to add when Lana tensed up. "We've been so focused on Audrey's death, we've hardly talked about your relationship. Do you know what you are going to do?"

"I think I finally do. Your pep talk made me realize that my ex-husband's lies were fundamentally different. Ron was cheating on me with another woman; Alex lied about taking part in several demonstrations because he was concerned I would be worried about his safety. His lies are insignificant in comparison to Ron's. Which means we must be able to find a way forward, at least, if he's still interested in trying."

"Considering how often he's called me and Dotty this past week, I would say he is definitely open to making it work."

"Good. I have to let my anger and hurt feelings towards Alex go, so we can move on. The bottom line is, I cannot imagine my life without him. And I don't want to," Lana said with a smile. The light at the end of the tunnel was getting brighter by the minute.

"I'm so glad to hear you say that." Willow wrapped her up in a bear hug. "Everything is going to work out with Alex, I just know it. Now all we have to do is figure out what to do about Wanderlust Tours."

Lana's grin faded in a heartbeat. "You said Dotty was open to me leading tours again."

"That was before someone else died in your presence—and on an organized tour, no less."

Lana felt tears forming in her eyes. "You don't think she'll—"

"Right after it happened, I didn't think it would be an issue, but how can Dotty ignore the facts? A tourist was murdered during a tour you were on. Of course Dotty is going to be concerned. Heck, it's freaking me out a little."

"This can't be happening!" Lana threw her head in her hands.

Willow leaned in. "I have a wild theory that might get you out of this mess. Hear me out, okay?"

Lana nodded.

"What if we've been looking at the deaths on your tours the wrong way?" Willow's tone was urgent. "What if you aren't an angel of death, but a guardian angel?"

Lana groaned. "Oh, please…"

"Lana, you saved my Jane from wrongful arrest, even when the Parisian police were certain she killed that guest. Maybe it's how your brain is wired. What if you are put into these positions in order to help protect the innocent? That being Elaine, in this case."

"My solving those murders had more to do with me being at the right place at the right time than my detective skills."

"Then we are certainly in the right place to solve this one. Without your help, Elaine will probably be arrested for Audrey's murder. She doesn't have a rich daddy who can swoop in and save her, and once the bridesmaids fly back to the States, I can imagine the Icelandic police will have no reason to keep looking for the real killer."

"You have the same access to the women that I do," Lana grumbled.

"Yes, but not the track record for solving murders." Willow grinned. "And now we have a chance to try to solve it together, with all the clues at our disposal."

"But why should we bother? I came here to get away from this kind of drama, not to get involved with another murder investigation."

"Maybe this is your destiny. Maybe you were meant to be on this trip in order to help Elaine."

Lana cocked her head as she studied her friend's expression. She knew from experience that once Willow got an idea in her head, it was almost impossible to get it out again. As much as Lana usually loved how persistent her dear friend was, being on the other side was less pleasant. "You want to play detective, don't you?"

"Yes, but I see myself more as Watson to your Sherlock." When Lana shook her head resolutely, Willow slapped her knee. "Come on, it's the only way to test my guardian angel theory—you have to try to free Elaine."

"Do I have to?" Lana locked eyes with her best friend, who slowly nodded her head. "I don't want to be anyone's guardian angel. I'd rather live my life murder-free."

"I see little other choice, especially if you want to keep your job. We have to figure out why this keeps happening to you. If not for Dotty's sake—for your own."

Lana's face drained of color. "You make a good point."

Willow slapped her hands together and began rubbing vigorously. "Alright, how do you usually start your investigation?"

"Let's see…I make a list of suspects and possible motives, then I try to interview everyone as casually as possible and hope they slip up. If that doesn't help me solve it, then I see what I can find out about the suspects online."

"Okay, when we get back to the hotel, making a list will be our first task." Willow grinned. "This is so exciting!"

Lana wished she felt the same exhilaration that Willow did. All she felt was dread at being dragged into another murder investigation.

23

Buckets of Rain

Lana could barely see the front of the boat as it cruised back to harbor. "It's a shame about the weather, but I am glad we got to see so many puffins."

"Indeed, although next time I go on vacation, it will be to somewhere warm and less rainy," Willow said.

The thunder and lightning brought buckets of rain. They raced from the boat to the company's headquarters, but their jackets were still soaking wet. They were ushered into a waiting room while the staff conferred. A few minutes later, the captain returned to the group of thirty-five tourists.

"We had hoped to continue further into the bay to search for whales, but the weather has been worsening all morning and it's just not safe to sail right now."

Groans of disappointment ringed the room.

"We can try to complete the whale-watching portion of the tour in about two hours, when the worst of the storm should have passed. But I cannot guarantee you that we will be able to depart. It all depends on how intense the storm is at that time. Otherwise, we can offer you tickets for another tour departing later this week. The guides will come around in a moment to ask which you would prefer."

The room was abuzz as the tourists conferred with each other, debating the pros and cons.

"What would you like to do, Lana?"

"Honestly, I'm feeling a little seasick. Would you mind skipping it today?"

Willow nodded vigorously. "Sounds good to me. My stomach is still doing somersaults. Let's see how the weather is tomorrow, and then decide."

"Perfect. What do you want to do with the rest of our afternoon? We could explore more of Reykjavik, but the weather's not exactly motivating me to take a long walk around the city center."

"No, it's not that inviting right now. I think we should start investigating Audrey's murder, so you can get your job back."

"You are actually looking forward to it, aren't you?"

"A little, I admit it." Willow blushed. "It's not the investigation that I'm excited about. It's the idea of helping to free someone who's been wrongly accused of a crime. That sounds thrilling."

Lana shivered. "Maybe the first few times. But my death tally is at eleven, and the excitement wore off long ago."

24

Watson and Sherlock On The Case

The shuttle bus back to the hotel rocked back and forth almost as much as their boat, convincing Lana and Willow to return to their room, instead of talking through their list of suspects in a local café.

"Where do we start?" Willow asked, her eyes twinkling. She and Lana were stretched out on one of the hotel room beds, with a laptop set up in-between them.

"The bachelorette party is a good start." Lana smoothed down the top page of her notebook, wishing she didn't have to use it to compile a list of suspects again. Knowing Willow was waiting for her to begin, she wrote down a list of names. "So, we have Elaine, Tabitha, Destiny, and Bianca."

"Don't forget Aunt Maureen and Gunnar," Willow said.

"Got it—anyone else?"

"The waitresses and cooks?" Willow offered.

"If it is a local, then we have no chance of solving this, but we can investigate the rest. As far as clues go, the police found Audrey's medical bracelet so we know that she is allergic to penicillin. And they also found Elaine's pill bottle, now mostly empty."

"And all of the bachelorettes claim they did not know that Audrey was allergic to penicillin. And Elaine said her medicine bottle was full when she arrived in Iceland. We should write that down."

"Check and check," Lana said as she finished making notations and then smiled up at her friend. "Okay, we are ready."

She looked down at her notebook. "First up is Elaine. Do you think she did it?"

"Not really. She just doesn't have the killer vibe."

"And the other bridesmaids do?"

"More than Elaine."

"Alright, I'll mark her as a maybe."

"I'd say probably not," Willow interjected.

"Next up, Tabitha."

Willow frowned. "What motive does she have, other than having a crush on Gunnar?"

"All three blondes do seem to melt in his presence."

"Gunnar is a ladies' magnet—and he can't seem to turn off his charm."

"I'll mark her as a maybe, too."

"Seriously? She and Elaine are off the list, just like that?"

"No, 'maybe' means we have to look them up online to see if they might have a hidden motive. But, as far as we know, neither woman had an obvious motive to kill their friend."

Willow nodded. "Alright, that makes sense." She peeked at Lana's notebook. "Destiny is our next suspect, and I think she is a viable one."

"Why do you think that?"

"She used to date Gunnar but now claims to be in love with a Spanish man that none of her friends have met. And now that Audrey's gone, Gunnar has fallen back into her arms. If he does inherit Audrey's money, then Destiny gets the guy and the money."

"That's a strong motive," Lana said as she jotted a few notes down.

"Should we look her up online now?" Willow asked.

"We can do that later. It's pretty time-consuming, and I'd like to get your opinion on our suspects, first," Lana said, feeling strange that she was again speaking from experience. She glanced at her notebook before asking, "What do we think about Bianca?"

"She was jealous of anyone who got close to Audrey and obviously likes Gunnar. But he does not seem to be into her."

Lana frowned. "No, he does not. She's a maybe, in my book." She tapped on her notebook. "Aunt Maureen is next. Now she is a piece of work."

"She does seem like a strong suspect to me," Willow confirmed. "And she did show up at the hotel just before Audrey collapsed."

"But she wasn't at the dinner," Lana pointed out.

"But she could have poisoned Audrey with something that took time to kill her. Did she touch Audrey, or hand her something? It could have been a slow-acting poison on an envelope or gift, and not the penicillin."

Lana raised an eyebrow at her friend. "Honey, you have been watching too much *CSI*."

"True," Willow said. "It's one of the only things on in the afternoons during Zoe's naps. I should probably read a book, instead."

"Okay, last up is Gunnar. He certainly gains the most by Audrey's death."

"And now he will get the money and the house, without the hassle of being tied down to one woman," Willow added.

"I doubt he'll be alone for long. But there is no way he could have poisoned her—he wasn't even at the hotel."

"But he may have known about Audrey's allergy to penicillin," Willow interjected.

"Why is that?"

"If he spent the night at her place, which I assume he did, he probably came across Audrey's medical bracelet in her bedroom or medicine cabinet. If he knew about it, he could have told one of the others."

"That's an excellent point, Willow," Lana said as she regarded her friend. "So he could have been involved in her murder, although that means he must have had a partner in crime."

"And by the looks of things, it could be any of the three bridesmaids. I don't think he and Aunt Maureen are working together—they act more like they want to drink each other's blood!"

"I concur," Lana said before throwing her pen across the notebook. "Well, that's it. Those are all of our main suspects and possible motives."

"It's not much to go on. What should we do next?"

"We could look them up online and see if we find anything new, but that might take all night. Or we could talk to the bridesmaids and see if they slip up and drop a clue."

"I vote for talking to the bridesmaids first," Willow said. "Bianca and Tabitha seemed pleased that Elaine is in police custody. They are so arrogant and self-centered that if they are involved, I wouldn't put it past them to say something incriminating, just to prove that they are untouchable."

25

Eager Investigators

"Alright, then finding the bachelorettes is our priority," Lana said.

"How are we going to split them up?"

"What do you mean?"

"In detective shows, the cops always question their suspects individually and then look for contradictions in their statements. That's how they usually solve the case."

Lana chuckled. "We aren't detectives, and this is not a TV show. If the opportunity presents itself, we can try to question them individually. But in reality, they have no reason to talk to us, especially about the murder. We'll have to try to be as casual as we can, which means if they are all together, then we will have to question them as a group."

Willow looked crestfallen. "Are you sure? Can't we try to create a distraction or invent an excuse to pull one aside?"

"If we seem too eager or pushy, they are going to clam up or chase us off. We aren't on tour anymore so there is no real reason for us to hang out together."

When Willow bit her lip, Lana added, "But we can approach them as concerned citizens who were also traumatized by Audrey's death. We can offer our condolences and ask how they are holding up, especially since one of their group was arrested for the murder."

A wide smile lit up Willow's face. "Bingo. Let's go find us some

129

bachelorettes."

Their search proved in vain because all three women were at the police station, according to the hotel's receptionist. At least, they had ordered a cab to take them there an hour earlier and weren't back yet. None of the hotel workers knew when the women were expected to return.

"What do you think—should we hang out here and wait for them, or do some sightseeing and try again later?" Willow asked.

"My vote is for a walk around the city. It is wet and windy, but we're from the Pacific Northwest so we can handle it. If we wait for the weather to clear up, we may never see more of Reykjavik," Lana said. "The bachelorettes aren't going to be checking out of the hotel tonight. Audrey's wedding was supposed to take place tomorrow afternoon, but from what I read online, it's now a memorial service for her. I have to assume that they will be going to that."

"Fair enough," Willow said, though Lana could hear the disappointment in her voice. She knew her friend was itching to play detective. Willow frowned at the weather before adding, "Let me grab a thicker jacket. It's raining pretty hard—even according to Seattle standards."

When she returned to the lobby a few minutes later, hail thundered down so hard, it was impossible to see the street running in front of the hotel.

"I know we are both used to heavy precipitation, but this is ridiculous. Can I buy you a coffee?" Lana said in a loud voice to be heard over the hail pounding on the roof.

"Yes, please. We don't see this kind of hail in the Pacific Northwest very often."

"True, it usually just drizzles all day long."

They found a table close to a window where they could try to make out Reykjavik's most famous sites through the brief breaks in the sheets of rain. In the distance, even through the heavy precipitation, they could make out the outline of the Hallgrimskirkja Church, its distinctive tower rising high above the city center. As the tallest building in downtown Reykjavik, it dominated the skyline.

"That is where Audrey was set to marry," Lana remarked. "I guess tomorrow it will be decorated for a funeral, instead."

"I suppose so," Willow replied, but Lana could tell she wasn't interested in talking about Audrey right now. Instead, they had a wonderful chat about Willow's family. It was obvious that she was really missing Jane and Zoe, which made Lana glad that her friend would be flying home soon.

However, the thought that Willow's trip may have been in vain saddened her. She still had to call Alex and see how receptive he was to working things out. And thanks to Audrey's murder, her ability to do her job was once again in question. Lana feared that Willow would leave before either situation was resolved.

"That latte was delicious. I wouldn't mind another one. The weather's not exactly clearing up," Willow said with a nod towards the window. Gusts of wind were blowing the trees from side to side as tiny tornadoes of cups and plastic bags raced through the streets. "At least we will have more time to figure out how to break the bad news to Dotty."

"That makes the next round my treat." Lana sprung up before Willow could protest. "I have to go to the ladies' room, so I can order the drinks on the way. Be right back."

When Lana returned a few minutes later, she heard three familiar voices standing by the bar before she saw their bottle-blonde hair. Tabitha, Destiny, and Bianca were dripping wet and their normally perfect makeup was streaked down their faces.

"Gunnar says he'll drive over after he's done with his family," Bianca said as she stared at her telephone's screen, apparently reading a text message aloud to her friends.

"He's going to need some tender loving care when he gets here," Tabitha purred. "I can't wait to comfort him."

"If he turns to anyone, it will be me. We used to date, remember?" Destiny snapped.

"Why not me? I've known Audrey longer. It should be me comforting him," Tabitha groused.

They are like sharks fighting over their prey, Lana thought. As much as she wanted to ignore them and walk past, Lana knew Willow would only send her right back. So she did the only thing she could think of. "Ladies, I'm sorry for your loss."

The three women turned in unison.

"Oh, it's the tour guide," Tabitha mumbled.

"Thanks, that's really sweet," Destiny added.

Lana made a show of looking around them. "Oh, I thought Elaine was with you. Or is she still in custody?"

"I don't know," Tabitha replied.

Lana frowned. "Weren't you just at the police station?"

"Yeah, to talk to Gunnar, not Audrey's killer," Bianca snapped. "He was helping the police with their investigation, and we wanted to see if he needed anything from us. We didn't ask about Elaine."

"And did he?"

"No, he's got everything under control."

"How is he holding up?"

All three women's faces turned to masks of sympathy.

"As well as can be expected," Bianca said.

"Losing your fiancée the night before your wedding would be tough on anyone," Destiny added.

"We will make sure he gets over her," Tabitha added, garnering stares from the rest.

"Don't you mean that we'll help him get through this difficult time?" Destiny asked.

Tabitha shrugged. "Sure, it's the same thing really."

"I guess I don't understand why the police are still holding Elaine," Lana said, pretending to be confused.

"Because she killed Audrey," Bianca exclaimed.

Willow had been watching them from their table, but crossed over to join the conversation. "But why would she harm Audrey? Elaine seemed to like her and detest Gunnar."

Lana hoped her friend wasn't pushing too hard.

"They say opposites attract, and, well, I think she hoped the old saying was true," Tabitha sniggered.

"Elaine did like what Audrey did for her, but I don't know if they were truly friends," Destiny said.

"What do you mean?" Lana asked.

"Audrey was letting Elaine sleep in the servants' quarters for free," Destiny explained.

"That cottage is larger than my apartment! It's more like a free-standing house," Bianca added. "When Audrey fired her, Elaine lost her paycheck and home. That had to hurt."

"I can imagine she was really mad about losing both, but killing Audrey wouldn't help her get either back," Willow reasoned.

"I don't know—maybe she was so overwhelmed by anger that she lashed out without thinking it through. I bet she knew that Audrey was allergic to penicillin and lied to the police about it," Tabitha said.

The others nodded in agreement.

"But none of you knew about her allergy?" Lana asked.

"Nope," Bianca replied.

"Did any of you see one of the waitresses put anything into Audrey's food or drink?" Lana asked, changing tactics.

"Of course not. If we had, we would have told the police," Tabitha said, a frown slowly forming on her face.

"Wasn't the aunt going to be evicted, as well, as soon as Audrey got back from her honeymoon? She was also at the hotel the night of the murder," Willow added.

"True, but she'll still get an allowance, at least if she is innocent of Audrey's murder," Destiny said. "That's for the police to decide, but they did release her from custody this morning, so I guess she's no longer a suspect."

"We all overhead Maureen saying that Gunnar wasn't right for her. What do you think, Destiny—were they good together? I assume you know him pretty well because you two used to date," Lana asked in as innocent of a tone as she could muster.

"What are you looking at me for? We did go out a few times, but it didn't last long. He and Audrey had a real connection, and I was nothing but happy for the two of them. Besides, why would I want Gunnar back—I'm in love with Pedro," Destiny said.

Bianca held up a manicured finger. "Wait a second—are you interrogating us?"

"No, I'm just curious by nature. I guess that's why I used to be a journalist," Lana admitted then immediately cringed, realizing too late her mistake.

Bianca rose and sprung back from the table. "Are you two undercover journalists? I bet they are wired—don't say anything else, ladies! Is this some sort of setup? We didn't do anything!"

"I don't want my name in any newspaper, not in connection with Audrey's murder," Tabitha gasped.

"Lana used to work for a newspaper, but that was years ago," Willow explained.

"Stay away from me and my friends!" Tabitha shrieked.

"We don't mean any harm!" Lana said.

"Leave us alone!" Destiny replied, standing in solidarity with the other two bridesmaids. The three glared at Lana and Willow as they walked backwards towards their table by the window. Before they sat down, Bianca pointed two fingers towards her eyes, then at Lana, gesturing that she would be watching the pair.

26

Faked Photographs

Only after they had paid their bill and returned to their hotel room did Lana dare to speak about the bachelorettes. "That went well."

"Maybe we were a little too pushy," Willow admitted. "But it was worth a shot."

"I guess, but I bet that will be our only chance to talk to them. There's no way they will let us question them again, at least not voluntarily." Lana flopped onto the couch, and Willow sat down next to her.

"One of them must be lying, but who?"

"My money is still on Destiny. Something about her relationship with Pedro just doesn't ring true."

"And Gunnar's been by her side since he arrived and she seems happy to let him cry on her shoulder," Willow added.

"It didn't sound like Pedro ever visited Destiny, so none of her friends have met him. And she acted really strange when Audrey talked about the Alhambra. I almost got the feeling she was lying about having been in Spain. I suppose it would be easy enough to make up a relationship, especially if it only consisted of a few photos or online posts," Lana said. "We could check her social media…"

"Let's do it!"

"But we don't know her last name. I guess we've hit a dead end."

Willow tapped her chin. "We could ask the hotel, or see if Audrey tagged

135

Destiny in any posts. It sounds like the wedding was big news back in the States. I can imagine Audrey posted about it on social media."

Sure enough, Audrey had tagged all of her bridesmaids on her Facebook and Instagram accounts. A quick look at Destiny's social media presence made clear that she did have a new boyfriend. Lana and Willow took in the handful of photos of Destiny and a dark-skinned gentleman kissing and cuddling in front of famous buildings in Barcelona, Madrid, and Cordoba.

"That answers that. She looks in love to me. And good for her—he's really handsome," Lana said.

"Hold your horses. There's something strange about that shot of them in front of the La Sagrada Familia. Let me just..." Willow zoomed in on the photo and studied it intently. A few moments later, her face lit up with a smile.

"Aha! Do you see how the shadows don't line up here and here?" She pointed out several spots on the image, in which the shadows of the church and couple were visible.

"Yeah, that is strange. But what does it mean?"

"I've been creating a lot of social media images for my studio lately and gotten pretty good with Photoshop. I bet you money that this photo is a composite!"

"And that is..." Lana looked up at her with a puzzled expression.

"That's when you take two photos and combine them into one. You have to pay attention to how each photograph is lit, or do a lot of touchup work to make the shadows line up, otherwise it's easy to tell that it's a composite. That would explain why these shadows don't match up—they are two different images lit from different angles. Which means Destiny probably wasn't in Barcelona, at least not with this guy." Willow tapped the screen with her fingernail.

"If it's even her boyfriend," Lana cried out. "It might just be a friend who posed with her for fun. But there's at least twenty pictures of them in Spain. Why would she go to all that trouble?"

"I don't know. There is one more thing that jumps out at me on her social media. Did you notice that there are no snaps of her and Gunnar?"

"Maybe she didn't take any. She said they didn't date long."

"Perhaps, but considering how many photos they have been taking of each other during this trip, you would think she would have posted at least one shot with him," Willow reasoned. "Maybe she deleted them all so the police wouldn't find out that she and Gunnar were once involved? Or maybe it was a way to convince Audrey that she was over Gunnar and in love with someone else?"

"Which means she might not be over Gunnar, after all." Lana stared at the photograph, a knot forming in her stomach as a horrifying thought entered her mind. "Have you ever read *Death on the Nile?*"

Willow raised an eyebrow. "That mystery by Agatha Christie? I saw the film. What of it?"

"What if Destiny and Gunnar didn't really break up? Maybe they lied about not being together, so that Gunnar could sweep Audrey off her feet, get her to change her will, and then kill her for the money? These photos and that story about Pedro might be part of a devious and long-term plan to set Audrey up, so Gunnar and Destiny could live happily ever after."

"Wait a second—you mean that Gunnar seduced Audrey with the intention of killing her as soon as she made him her beneficiary?"

Lana's nose crinkled. "Yeah, it does sound pretty silly."

"No—it sounds exactly right!" Willow squealed. "Them not breaking up makes perfect sense. Which means those lies about Pedro were just a diversion to make Audrey think Destiny found a new love. We should tell the police."

Lana shifted uncomfortably in her seat. "I guess we could tell them that they used to be a couple, but we can't accuse anyone of murder. We don't have any evidence of foul play, only a few suspicious photographs."

Willow threw up her hands. "We have to do something! Elaine's supposed friends are certainly happy to let her hang. And I know you don't want to see an innocent person jailed for something they did not do. We both know Elaine could not have done this—"

"Do we? We hardly know these young women. Elaine could have been lying to us the whole time and we wouldn't know it."

"She is so down to earth compared to the rest. All I'm saying is we should tell the detective that Gunnar and Destiny once dated. Then he can take it from there."

"When you say it like that, it doesn't sound like we have much of a choice. Their relationship could be important to the case."

Willow picked up the hotel room phone and handed it to Lana. "Why don't you call him? You've got more experience with this kind of thing."

Lana grabbed the receiver, knowing her friend was right.

Under Willow's watchful eye, she explained to the detective what they had discovered and asked whether he knew Gunnar and Destiny had once dated. She turned the phone's receiver so Willow could listen to his response.

"Yes, both were quite forthcoming about that fact. But they are both in relationships with different people now. I see no motive," was his tart reply before he hung up on her.

"Okay, so he already knew about them dating," Lana said.

"Hmmm, alright. Should we take a look online and see what we can find out about the others?"

"Why not? The way the wind is whipping past our window, I don't think the weather's lightened up."

Lana pulled out her laptop, and they sat on the bed so both could easily see the screen. A few minutes later and they were glancing over Tabitha's plentiful social media posts.

"She goes through men like Kleenex!" Willow exclaimed as they scrolled past another of Tabitha's posts featuring her latest beau. It looked like she had a new boyfriend every month, and the only thing they had in common was a healthy bank account. In the carefully constructed photos, Tabitha was drinking champagne on rooftop balconies, jet skiing in Florida, showing off diamond-encrusted jewelry, diving in the Caribbean, and posing in string bikinis on several different yachts.

"I want her life," Willow mumbled as they scrolled past a shot of Tabitha disembarking from a private jet.

"She sure does enjoy the high life. I don't see her having any money issues, nor does she have a problem finding a date. So why would she murder to be with Gunnar?"

"He is undeniably sexy and a billionaire, at least once he inherits from Audrey."

"True, then Tabitha would have the best of both worlds. But Gunnar isn't exactly falling into her arms. Destiny's the only one he's been turning to, so far as I can tell."

"That could be because he doesn't want to attract attention to their relationship," Willow said tentatively.

Lana pursed her lips at the screen. "I supposed, but I still think Destiny's a stronger suspect."

"I agree, but I don't want to discount the others quite yet. What about Bianca? Is there anything juicy to find out about her?"

"I hope so. I really don't like her," Lana grumbled.

"I know what you mean, she really grates on my nerves."

Moments later, they were looking over a map of San Francisco. "It is creepy how much personal information you can find about someone online," Willow said as Lana zoomed in until one street filled the screen.

"True, but in this case, it sure is handy that Bianca and Gunnar's family keep their Facebook profiles up to date." Lana nodded to the screen. "Here is Bianca's family home."

She then opened another browser window and pulled up the same map. However this time, she zoomed in on another address. "And this is where Gunnar's parents lives."

The pair stared at the two homes, located mere blocks from each other in the same gated community just outside of San Francisco.

"They grew up three blocks apart," Willow exclaimed.

"Indeed. So this proves they must have known of each other, but that doesn't necessarily mean they were friends before they moved up to Portland. Though it does increase the odds," Lana muttered as she stared at the map. "Didn't Elaine say something about how rich families tend to stick together? We'll have to ask Bianca about it."

"It is strange how Bianca starts to drool when he walks in the room, but Gunnar is not exactly nice to her."

"That's a good point. If she has a crush on him, he could have used it to make her do his bidding."

"Would you kill someone because they asked you to?" Willow asked.

"No, but everybody is different, I've learned. It's hard to tell what would trigger a person to kill." Lana chewed on her lip, considering their list of suspects. "Who do you think poisoned Audrey?"

Willow stared at the screen for a moment. "I guess Destiny is our best candidate. I would like to know why she posted all of those fake photos."

"How are we going to figure that out without talking to her again? And even if we get her to admit it, I can't imagine those pictures are enough evidence for the police to arrest her."

"We could confront her at the memorial service," Willow said.

"What! Why would we go to that?"

"Technically we did know Audrey, so no one would question us wanting to pay our respects."

When her forehead creased, Willow grabbed her arm. "Come on, it's addictive, Lana! I feel like an actual sleuth, sifting through the clues, in search of the truth."

"Try playing Clue," she mumbled. "It's a game, so no one dies for real."

Willow ignored her. "And if it helps us prove that Elaine is innocent, then we also help you get your job back. Dotty won't be able to deny that you are a guardian angel instead of a murder magnet, if we do. It's a win-win."

"As long as we don't put ourselves in harm's way," Lana begged. "I couldn't live with myself if you got injured."

"Agreed." Willow stuck out her hand.

Lana sighed. "I guess we're attending a memorial service. I only hope I have something appropriate to wear."

27

Memorializing Audrey

Friday—Reykjavik, Iceland

The official memorial service honoring Audrey's life was held in the Hallgrimskirkja Church, one of Iceland's most iconic buildings thanks to its soaring height and unique shape. As the tallest building in downtown Reykjavik, it dominated the city skyline.

A statue of Leifur Eiriksson, dressed in clothes reminiscent of a Viking, stood on a tall pedestal just outside the entrance. The church's wide façade seemed to be constructed from rows of thin stone pillars placed close together. Rising from the center was the church's tower, also covered with jagged white pillars. Lana had read that the Icelandic architect was inspired by the country's natural and geological beauty and often used columns of basalt, the country's most common geological feature, in his work.

They arrived a bit late, but the ceremony had apparently not yet begun, for a long line of mourners still snaked out of the main entrance. Willow and Lana joined the slow-moving queue that led past Gunnar and his parents, allowing visitors to convey their personal condolences before taking their seats.

Soon they were inside the church. It was one of the most sparsely decorated religious institutions Lana had ever seen, yet it was not a somber space. The lack of decoration made the ceilings seem even taller, and the many windows even larger.

When it was their turn to speak to Gunnar's parents, Lana said with as much emotion as she could, "I am so sorry for your loss. Audrey was far too young."

"Yes, well, they made a beautiful couple. It's really too bad things ended up as they did," answered Gunnar's mother with a shrug.

Lana wouldn't categorize the older woman's tone as flippant, but Gunnar's mother was surprisingly unemotional about Audrey's death. His father only nodded then looked past them, towards the next group of mourners.

After they had passed, Willow whispered to Lana, "Her son's fiancée is poisoned and all she can do is shrug her shoulders?"

"Maybe not showing your emotions in public is an Icelandic thing."

"I guess, which means Gunnar is as all-American as you can get," Willow said with a nod ahead. Gunnar stood a few feet away, and in comparison to his parents, he seemed almost inconsolable. He sobbed openly, allowing a number of female mourners to comfort him.

"Maybe we should skip speaking to him and find a place to sit. Preferably somewhere where we can keep an eye on Destiny." Of the three bridesmaids, Lana still considered her the most likely to be working with Gunnar. If the two of them were in cahoots, she only hoped that one or both would slip up and make a mistake today. If not, he and the bachelorettes would all fly home tomorrow, and Elaine would most likely be charged with the crime, leaving Lana forever wondering whether the Icelandic police had Audrey's true killer in custody.

"I don't see the bridesmaids, but I bet they will be seated at the front, with the family. Let's see if we can find anything close by."

Willow pointed to a few free seats two rows behind the "family only" pew, just as a cry made them look towards the entrance of the church. Audrey's aunt had burst inside and was pointing a finger at Gunnar.

"You killed my niece for money, but it won't work!" Maureen's words ricocheted around the church. "My lawyers assure me that you will inherit nothing! You aren't entitled to her money because you weren't married yet. Everything goes to charities now."

"You're just trying to scare me off. Audrey promised me everything." Gunnar began charging towards her, when his mother yelled out his name before speaking rapidly to him in Icelandic. Whatever she said made him stop in his tracks, but his expression remained livid.

"You should have waited until after you were married before you had your girlfriend poison her," Maureen taunted Gunnar as she glared at Destiny.

"I didn't do it!" Destiny cried.

"See, even the aunt thinks Destiny is the killer," Willow mumbled.

"Audrey told me I would inherit everything," Gunnar repeated, his tone resolute. "I'm done talking to you. Our lawyers can battle it out. Today, I am mourning my wife."

"I will not rest until justice is served!" Maureen screamed before two beefy mourners escorted her back outside.

"Why is Gunnar so focused on the money? His own family may not be as rich as Audrey was, but they must still be worth several million," Willow said.

"On paper, maybe," Lana mused. "But what if Maureen is right and they are about to file for bankruptcy? With Audrey's money, they could pay off their loans and keep expanding. Without it, they go under."

"What a horrible reason to take a life."

Gunnar's parents circled around him, talking to him until his anger subsided. Only then did they take their places at the front pew.

The official memorial service was surprisingly simple and short. Other than the three bridesmaids, only Gunnar rose to speak about Audrey. However, he quickly succumbed to his emotions and Destiny had to lead him off the stage. In Lana's book, the fact that she was rubbing his back and whispering in his ear made her theory even more plausible.

"She doesn't even try to hide her feelings for him," Willow whispered.

As soon as the official ceremony ended, those who wished to attend the wake were ushered into minibuses that whisked them a few blocks away, to where the more informal event was taking place.

Lana and Willow searched the crowd for the three bridesmaids, curious to see whether they had latched onto Gunnar or not. All three were pulling on their jackets and walking towards the line of mourners waiting for the buses.

"Are we going to join them?"

"Do we have a choice? We need to figure out if one of the others did this, before everyone flies home. I don't know how Dotty will react, otherwise. If you really are a guardian angel, then you should be able to solve this," Willow reasoned.

"No pressure," Lana smirked. "Alright, let's get in line."

The three bridesmaids boarded the bus before theirs. Not that it mattered; a few minutes later they were already disembarking and rushing into a large glass-enclosed restaurant located on the waterfront close to the Old Harbor. Visibility was a bit better than yesterday, but the weather was still not clear. Instead of buckets of rain, it felt more like someone had forgotten to turn off the shower.

A long buffet had been set up along one wall, providing enough food and drink to satisfy several hundred guests. Round tables, each large enough to seat eight, dotted the floor.

"They must have invited more people to this reception than were at the church," Willow noted.

"It sure looks like it," Lana said. "Which is even more reason to find the bridesmaids and get this interrogation over with. Once this place fills up, it's going to be difficult to keep track of them."

They meandered around the rapidly filling hall, until Lana spotted their targets. The three blondes had already ditched their jackets and were sitting at a table close to the back of the hall, staring at their phones.

While Lana tried to figured out which tactic to use to get close to them, Willow had already decided on the direct approach.

She charged up to the bridesmaids and hissed, "You all lied to us. We know one of you killed Audrey!"

"Keep your voice down! What are you talking about? None of us harmed her; we loved her." Tabitha waved Willow into one of the seats.

"If you haven't noticed, we are at our best friend's memorial service. Can you save the crazy for another time?" Bianca added.

Her snarky grin seemed to strengthen Willow's resolve. "Bianca, you and Gunnar grew up in the same gated community, but you two acted like strangers. What gives?"

Bianca shifted uncomfortably in her seat as Tabitha and Destiny stared at her.

"We didn't know you two grew up together," Tabitha finally said.

"I didn't get the impression that he liked having you around," Destiny added.

"Hundreds of families live there. Just because we grew up in the same community doesn't mean we were close. I knew of Gunnar, but he and I never really hung out in the same circles. He and his parents are real snobs and always thought they were better than most of the families living there," Bianca confided.

"Besides, if you think I poisoned Audrey, then you really are bonkers. I'm the one who tried to save her from slipping off the waterfall—remember?"

"Good point," Lana mumbled.

Willow turned her accusatory glare towards Tabitha, who immediately began shaking her head.

"Why would I kill Audrey? She paid for all of my clothes, shoes, and purses whenever we went shopping together. It's not like I'm in her will—none of us are."

"What about Gunnar—you couldn't keep your eyes off him, even when he was standing next to his bride-to-be!"

Tabitha waved Willow's comment away. "Gunnar is easy on the eyes, but no man is worth risking prison time for. Jailhouse orange is not a good look on me."

The pair of amateur detectives looked at each other and shrugged, before turning to Destiny.

The younger woman threw up her hands. "I bet you think Audrey stole Gunnar from me, but nothing is further from the truth! Gunnar was fun, but we only went out a few times, and I never had the impression that he was in love with me. He and Audrey really were destined to be married—who was I to stand in their way? And if I had stayed with Gunnar, I never would have met Pedro. He's my soulmate, I just know he is."

"If you two are so in love, why hasn't he flown over to visit you yet?" Tabitha asked.

"He's studying at the university," Destiny stuttered. "That's why I'm looking into how I can move over to Spain, permanently."

"Oh, you two are serious," Tabitha said.

"I have a plan—we'll see what happens. I'm not giving up on love, not yet."

"Speaking of which, could we talk to you—in private?" Lana said before Willow could expose her secret to the rest. If Destiny felt embarrassed or trapped, she might not tell them the truth.

When Lana noted Destiny's puzzled expression, she added, "It's about your photos of Pedro. Do you have a minute?"

Destiny shrugged at the others as she followed Lana away from Tabitha and Bianca.

"What is it?"

"We noticed that your photos of you and Pedro have been manipulated. You were never in Spain, were you?"

"Why were you looking at my social media?" Destiny demanded.

"We don't think Elaine killed Audrey."

"Well, I didn't do it!"

Destiny's eyes darted over to Bianca and Tabitha, still seated but clearly watching their conversation with interest. "Alright, I'll tell you the truth if you promise not to tell the others." She made eye contact and only continued after both Lana and Willow nodded.

"My dad's business went under a few months ago, and he can't find work. I think we're going to have to sell the house." Destiny sounded miserable. "I didn't go to Europe; I spent the summer in Fresno babysitting my cousins to make money."

Lana covered her mouth, hoping to hide her surprise. "Why did you lie to your friends?"

"My parents begged me not to tell anyone about Dad's business going bankrupt, but I couldn't disappear for the whole summer and not say anything to Audrey. She is one of my best friends. So I made up that lie about flying to Europe for the summer."

Destiny looked away and sighed. "Except I didn't expect to meet the man of my dreams. That's when things got complicated."

"How did you and Pedro meet?" Willow asked.

"His family lives next door to my cousins. He was home for the summer, and we got to know each other pretty well. He's a great guy and really smart. He's Hispanic, which is why I pretended he was from Madrid. I'm pretty good with Photoshop so I changed the background of a few photos so it looked like we were in Spain. They fooled Audrey, but apparently not you two."

"Is that why he hasn't flown up to meet your friends?"

"Partly. But it's more about the money than anything else. He just started a two-year master's at UCLA and can't afford to fly up to visit me. He's already working two jobs to pay for his studies and housing, as it is. Neither of us wants to be in a long-distance relationship, and I've got nothing tying me to Portland, so I'm looking for a job in Los Angeles."

"Why should we believe you?" Willow asked as she crossed her arms over her torso.

"But you must—I didn't hurt my friend!" Destiny grabbed her phone and scrolled quickly through her photos before turning her phone so that Lana and Willow could see. "Look—these are the original photos of us that I took in Fresno."

The passion with which she and Pedro kissed spattered off the tiny screen. If those two weren't in love, Lana didn't know who was.

"You're right, Destiny. It sure looks like you've found your true love. I hope you can find a way to get to Los Angeles. And by the way—he is gorgeous!"

Destiny's face lit up as she gazed at the photos of her boyfriend.

"So if you didn't do it, who do you think killed Audrey?" Willow dared to ask.

Destiny bit her lip and shook her head. "I'm really not sure. But that aunt of hers is so obsessed with maintaining her country club lifestyle. If she thought that she could still inherit if Audrey died before her wedding, I wouldn't put it past Maureen to try to knock her off. But she wasn't at the dinner, so I guess she couldn't have done it."

"True," Lana said, unwilling to share their theory with Destiny that perhaps two people had worked together to kill her friend.

"Do you think Gunnar was in love with Audrey?" Willow asked, her gaze fixed on the man in question.

Destiny looked over to Gunnar, surrounded by a gaggle of young women dressed in black. "I think he did love Audrey, but now that she's gone, he'll find someone else. He's not the kind of guy to dwell on the past."

28

Mourning a Friend

"Are we done here?" Destiny looked to Lana and Willow. "I am here to mourn my friend."

"Of course, sorry. Thanks for answering our questions," Lana said.

Destiny turned to walk away, but spun back on her heel to face the pair. "Why do you care? You didn't know Audrey or Elaine."

Willow blushed. "I guess it's an intellectual exercise."

"And Bianca was right when she said we are all suspects until the police make an arrest," Lana added.

"Didn't you hear? They officially arrested Elaine last night. It looks like her penicillin is what cost Audrey her life."

Lana's face drained of color. If she was Elaine's guardian angel, she'd mucked up pretty badly. "No, we hadn't heard that. Thanks for letting us know."

"So you can stop playing detective now, okay? It's freaking us all out. Can we just focus on celebrating Audrey's life today?" Destiny asked.

Lana threw a hand over her heart. "Sure thing, we promise to stay out of your hair."

Destiny nodded and gave them both a tiny grin before returning to the table where her friends had been sitting.

However, Lana noted that only Tabitha was still there. "Where did Bianca go?"

149

"Does it matter? Destiny is right; if Elaine has been arrested, the police must know something we do not. Which means this case is closed, right?" Willow said, the disappointment evident in her voice.

Lana threw an arm over her shoulder. "I'm sorry we didn't solve this one, Watson. But I am glad that neither one of us got hurt. And at least you helped me figure out what to do about Alex."

"But what about your job?"

"We'll see how Dotty reacts to the news, and then go from there."

"Sounds good. Now, do you want to leave or grab a drink? It's still raining outside, and the bar is open."

Lana chuckled as she looked towards the bar, and the long lines leading up to it.

"You know what—I would rather leave this whole Audrey situation behind. Why don't we get out of here and grab a drink in a local bar, instead?"

"That sounds like a far better plan."

They began walking back towards the exit, when an unexpected sight caught Lana's eye. Standing next to a pair of French doors that opened onto the terrace at the back of the building were Gunnar and Bianca, their heads close. She nudged her friend and pointed to the pair's location. "Are you seeing what I'm seeing?"

Willow stopped and stared. "Are he and Bianca kissing or arguing?"

"I'm not sure, but they are standing awfully close to be strangers. Is she whispering into his ear?"

Suddenly Gunnar threw up his arms, clearly enraged by something Bianca had said. When he turned to walk away, Bianca grabbed his shoulder and turned him back towards her. His head hung low as she stroked his arms and back.

"And that is far too intimate of a gesture to be strangers."

"Oh, my! Lana, what if your *Death on the Nile* theory is correct, but with a different couple?"

Before Lana could reply, Gunnar pushed Bianca's hands away and rushed out the doors and into the raging storm. Without hesitation, Bianca followed.

"There's only one way to find out. Come on!" Lana weaved through the crowd, focused on reaching the doors.

The wind was so strong, it whipped the rain sideways across their path, soaking them to the core in seconds. Lana shivered as she pushed on, following Bianca's shrill voice around the edge of the building and towards the coastline.

As soon as they turned the corner, their targets were in sight. Bianca and Gunnar were standing at the end of the restaurant's pier, stretching far into the choppy water. Bianca stood with her back to the shoreline as Gunnar continued his tirade. The strong winds whipped their voices towards Lana and Willow, enabling them to hear everything the pair was arguing about.

"You poisoned her too soon. What if Maureen is right and I inherit nothing? What are my parents going to do?"

"So the aunt was right—his family's business is about to go bankrupt," Willow exclaimed in a loud whisper to Lana. Luckily, they were far enough away that Gunnar and Bianca couldn't hear them.

"You wanted me to kill her before your wedding, remember?" Bianca insisted.

"I might have been wrong about the timing—we should have waited until after the wedding, just to be sure."

"Well it's a little late now, isn't it? I can't bring Audrey back, Gunnar." Bianca leaned in and grabbed his hand. "But we still have each other."

Gunnar tore his hand out of hers. "What? I never wanted you!"

"But you said you loved me and we'd be together, if I got rid of Audrey!"

"No, I said we would both get rich. But you acted too soon and now you can kiss your million dollars goodbye."

"How can you say that after all I did for you? I never wanted your money—I want you!"

"That was never part of the bargain, Bianca, and you know it."

"If you don't want to be with me, then I'm going to the police." Bianca threw her arms over her torso, as if that defiant gesture would protect her. But Gunnar was a bull about to charge, and Willow and Lana were too far away to do anything to stop him.

"Gunnar—the police know you two killed Audrey! They are right behind us!" Lana sprung up as she screamed, hoping her lies would be enough to stop him from harming Bianca.

Unfortunately, her words only seemed to enrage Gunnar further. He leaned down and charged at Bianca with his hands stretched out. Though she tried to dodge his grasp, he was far too fast. With one firm push of his hands, Bianca was in the choppy sea, bobbing for her life in ice-cold water.

"We have to help her—she won't last long out there!" Lana yelled.

Willow was already halfway to Bianca, who was splashing around the freezing water as she tried to make her way back to the ladder hanging off the dock. Unfortunately the strong currents were pushing her away from shore.

Gunnar was racing back up the dock when he darted to the left and tackled Willow, taking her down hard.

"Willow!" Lana screeched, her worst nightmare playing out before her eyes. If anything happened to her friend, she would never be able to forgive herself.

She rushed towards the pair now wrestling on the ground, intending to jump onto Gunnar's back. Before Lana could, her wiry friend wrapped her leg around Gunnar's and whipped him forward, throwing him off balance. He hit the ground hard, the thump clearly audible above the drizzling rain. Willow was not only a yoga teacher, she was also a black belt in karate.

As he hit the ground, Lana breathed a sigh of relief and raced past her friend. She scurried down the ladder, but stopped on the bottom rung. Jumping into the icy bay would only lead to more trouble. She held out her hand as far as she could, her legs already freezing in the cold water. Could Bianca still control her muscles in these temperatures?

"Grab onto my hand and I'll pull you in. Can you swim towards me?"

"I'll try," came the chattery response.

Bianca doggy-paddled her way close enough that Lana could grab her hand and pull her in. Willow helped her up the ladder, ice-cold water dripping off of her clothes. Bianca collapsed onto the pier and began shaking from, Lana assumed, the fright and cold.

"Can you help me get Bianca back inside?"

"Dang it!" Willow yelped, instead of helping to lift up the maid of honor. Lana looked up to see Gunnar racing down the shoreline.

"What about Gunnar? Shouldn't we run after him?" Willow asked. He was already hopping over the restaurant's perimeter fence and racing down the waterfront.

"He won't escape the police. He and his family are too well-known for him to hide out for long."

They turned to the blonde bridesmaid.

"Before we take Bianca back inside, I want some answers," Willow stated.

"Her teeth are chattering, Willow," Lana whispered.

"I don't care—Bianca deserves to suffer a little. She killed her good friend two days before her wedding. That's pretty cold to me. I want to know why she did it, and then we'll take her inside."

"I did for Gunnar," Bianca cried. "I've been in love with him since grade school, and he knows it. He told me if I killed Audrey, then we would buy a yacht and sail to Jamacia. What is more romantic than that?"

"Except for the killing part..." Lana grumbled.

"It was his idea to poison her, not mine," Bianca insisted.

"If you and Gunnar are working together, why did he push you in the water? Does he not want to share anymore?" Willow asked.

"He was mad because I killed her too soon. But he wanted Audrey to die here in Iceland, before they left for their honeymoon. He said it would be easier to get away with murder in a foreign country. Audrey's aunt doesn't have any connections here that she could call on to get involved with the case. And Gunnar said if I could knock her off in a way that could be considered an accident, it would be even easier to get away with it. Now that Maureen is fighting the change in Audrey's will tooth and nail, he's trying to shift the blame to me."

What disturbed Lana most was how calm and collected Bianca remained. Sure, her body trembled from the cold, but she showed no signs of regret or remorse. Only anger that Gunnar had betrayed her.

Something in Lana's brain clicked. "You were the one who encouraged her to step off the trail on the glacier, weren't you?"

Bianca nodded. "When that didn't work, I threw a stone at her head when she was about to get away from me at the waterfall. That knocked her in the water, but she managed to grab onto that rock. If I could have reached her hand, I could have gotten rid of her then and there, and everyone would have assumed it was an accident."

When she noted Lana and Willow's shocked expressions, Bianca added, "Don't expect me to admit that to the police—or any of this for that matter. You aren't cops and I'm going into hypothermic shock, so anything I say is delusional nonsense."

When Bianca began to cackle, Lana looked to Willow. "We better get her back inside and call the police. They can deal with this mess."

Willow shook her head at the bridesmaid. "You're a cold-blooded sociopath. I hope you get your due."

"No, I'm a woman scorned!" Bianca screamed. "Gunnar was just using me to do the dirty work, so all he has to do is mourn. That's what hurts the most—knowing he manipulated me into killing Audrey."

Lana cocked her head at the younger woman. "That's the line you are going to use with the police, isn't it?

She curled her lips. "Why not? It's true. Gunnar is quite controlling. And he lied about being rich—his whole family did. I guess he comes from a long line of liars. How can the police trust anything he says about me?"

Lana shook her head, saddened by the woman's mental condition. Was she a sociopath or simply mad with love? Aloud she asked, "But why? She was your friend."

Bianca blew out her cheeks. "Yeah, right. I only rode horses with Audrey because my uncle wanted me to suck up to her family. She was too stuck up to really be friends with anyone. I guess it was how her aunt raised her, but she wasn't able to be a part of any group—she had to be the best at everything."

"But why did you poison Audrey with penicillin during dinner? That couldn't have been an accident. Were you trying to frame Elaine, or was that a coincidence?" Willow asked.

"Oh, no, I wanted Elaine to take the fall. After Audrey uninvited her to her wedding, I knew I had to act fast. Gunnar had already told me that Audrey was allergic to penicillin, and when Elaine mentioned she was taking it, I figured it would be easy enough to frame her. I swiped a few of her pills, crushed them up, and kept the vial in my purse, in case the opportunity arose. And it did, during dinner. The others were so busy with their makeup, they didn't even notice me dumping it into Audrey's daiquiri."

"But I thought the puffin was poisoned," Willow said.

"Nope, but the timing was brilliant. Death by puffin sounds so much more intriguing than death by daiquiri."

"But why frame her? What did Elaine ever do to you?"

"Because she is not one of us. I couldn't let Destiny or Tabitha take the fall. I see their parents at the country club. But Elaine is expendable, as far as I'm concerned."

29

The Whole Truth

"Lana! Are you alright? You sound really upset."

"I'm fine. It is so good to hear your voice, Alex. I miss you." Lana fought back the tears forming in her eyes and catching at her throat. The last thing she wanted to do was burden him with another story about a murder. Right now, they had more important things to discuss.

"You know what," Lana continued, "I finally figured out what is most important in life—you and me, making it work. I love you far too much to let you go. Can we try again?"

"Yes, please!" Alex cried through the phone. "I love you so much, it hurts. I wish I could undo all the pain I caused. I promise to do whatever it takes to make things right. I'll even install one of those phone tracers, so you can track my movements, if that's what you want. I just can't lose you again."

"No more lies?" Lana whispered.

"No more lies," Alex stated resolutely. "From now on you get the whole truth, whether you like it or not."

Lana giggled, as relief and joy filled her soul. "Good."

"Speaking of the whole truth—there is something I need to tell you, instead of letting you hear it from Dotty." The hesitation in his voice set Lana on edge.

"As you know, I haven't been happy at my job, not for a long time. So I quit last week."

"You what?" Lana screeched, happy that he had quit a job he had grown to despise, but slightly terrified for his future prospects.

"Do you have any idea of what you are going to do next?"

"I do. I got involved with the Earth Warriors to break out of the slog of corporate life and have an adventure. So I found a new job that provides both."

"That sounds good. But what does Dotty have to do with any of this?"

"She's my new boss."

"Seriously? Are you going to work as a guide for Wanderlust Tours?" Lana was close to speechless. That was the last thing she had expected him to do.

"I can't let you have all the fun," he laughed, then added hastily, "Don't worry, I don't expect us to lead tours together—that might be too intense. But Dotty promised to schedule our free time so we could spend it together. Lately, it seems like every time I fly home from working a conference, you are leaving to fly out and lead a tour."

"That's true. But you know the city tours aren't that adventurous, right?"

"Dotty wants to start offering more adventure-oriented tours and offered me the chance to lead them."

"What do you mean? I'd never heard her mention wanting to do that," Lana mumbled, surprised he knew something that she did not.

"Sea kayaking in Belize, ski trips in the Alps, snorkeling in Fiji—that kind of thing. Dotty said she's had plans to create these new tours for a younger crowd but hadn't worked out the itineraries yet. Apparently, I've spurred her into action, and she's making them a priority."

"That sounds amazing! And the Earth Warriors?"

"I'm done with radical protesting. Donating money will be the limit of my involvement from now on. So are you coming home next, or are you off on another tour?" Alex blurted out, as if he'd finally gotten up the nerve to ask.

"I'm heading home. I miss Seymour."

"Oh, of course, your cat. He's not very good with phones. Should I see if he'll meow for you?"

"Come on, silly. I miss you, too, Alex."

He laughed. "Well, good! I haven't changed the locks, yet. And if you tell me when your flight arrives, I'll even pick you up from the airport."

"It's a deal!"

After they'd said their prolonged goodbyes, Lana lay back onto her hotel room bed and sighed. She was glad to know that at least one of the two crises in her life had found a happy resolution. Now all she had to do was call her boss, Dotty.

30

Finding Happiness

Saturday—Reykjavik, Iceland

Lana stared out the window, watching as squalls of driving rain pounded down on the coastline in front of them. "I wouldn't want to be outside, but it is quite spectacular."

"Indeed, this weather is pretty intense. I'm glad it's supposed to be calming down in a few hours. I would rather not have to fly out in this storm," Willow said before taking another sip of her tea.

They were in a café in Reykjavik, enjoying a fresh ginger and mint tea while they watched the most recent storm pass through. In five hours, they would be catching a plane back to Seattle. Dotty had not only paid for Lana's ticket home, she also bumped them both up to first class.

Hanging from one wall was a television broadcasting the local news. They couldn't understand Icelandic, but the pictures of Gunnar and Bianca in handcuffs spoke for themselves. It did help that they had already checked online and discovered that their arrests were international news. Gunnar's family was also mentioned in the reports due to this morning's announcement that John's Sporting Goods had filed for bankruptcy.

"It looks like Bianca wasn't able to shift all of the blame to Gunnar, like she thought."

"True. I still don't know why she thought that would work. Gunnar wasn't even at the hotel when Audrey was poisoned."

"According to the online news, the police played Gunnar and Bianca off of each other, so that he finally broke down and told them everything. It's so sad—it really was all about the money." Willow laid her phone down and looked Lana in the eye. "You do realize if we hadn't stuck our noses in, Elaine would still be in jail."

"That may be true, but I would prefer to stay out of any future police investigations—especially ones involving murder. What about you? You were so gung-ho to solve the case, and we did. Does it make you want to get your PI's license?" Lana teased.

"No way! It was thrilling enough taking part in this one, but I wouldn't want to make a job out of it. I'm still pretty sore from Gunnar's tackle. From now on, I'm sticking to Clue."

Lana raised her teacup. "Glad to hear it."

"So it sounds like you and Alex have kissed and made up. What did Dotty say last night?"

"To guide or not to guide, that is the question," Lana mused. "I think I found a way to keep traveling, but not have to worry about murderous clients, at least for a while."

Willow cocked her head. "What do you mean?"

"Dotty wants to add a new line of tours aimed at a younger, more backpacker-y crowd. She's looking for a few experienced guides to scout several locations in Asia and the Pacific Rim, and I convinced her to let me go on a few of the research trips for her. So it'll be me and a backpack for a few weeks. Which means less chance of dead bodies, I hope."

She looked to her friend. "I know you think I'm some sort of guardian angel, but I'd rather let someone else deal with the murders from now on."

"I get it. It sounds like you've found a way to travel again, and will have some time to rebuild your confidence before dealing with clients again. That's perfect!"

"Exactly. It will be a wonderful new challenge. And now that Alex and I have patched things up, I am finally starting to feel more positive about life again," Lana laughed.

Willow laid a hand over hers. "I am so glad to hear that, Lana. You truly deserve all the happiness in the world."

THE END

Thanks for reading *Death by Puffin*!

Reviews really do help readers decide whether they want to take a chance on a new author. If you enjoyed this story, please consider posting a review on BookBub, on Goodreads, or with your favorite retailer. I appreciate it!

Jennifer S. Alderson

Acknowledgements

I want to thank all of the readers who have encouraged me to continue writing the Travel Can Be Murder Cozy Mystery Series. It has been a pleasure to travel with Lana Hansen!

I also want to thank my wonderful family for helping me create the time and space to write during the many lockdowns and school closures that took place while I was writing this series.

My editor, Sadye Scott-Hainchek of The Fussy Librarian, has done an excellent job polishing this series, and I am grateful for her outstanding work and advice. As I am to Elizabeth Mackey, the cover designer for this series.

I will be taking a short break from writing more of Lana's adventures while I develop two more cozy mystery series that I hope you will enjoy as much as this one.

Spoiler alert—one will feature Randy Wright, Lana's good friend and a former guide for Wanderlust Tours! The second will be a combination of art thriller and cozy mystery that I hope will please fans of this series, and the Zelda Richardson Mysteries. I cannot wait to introduce you to these new stories and characters early next year.

Until then, happy reading and travels!

About the Author

Jennifer S. Alderson was born in San Francisco, raised in Seattle, and currently lives in Amsterdam. After traveling extensively around Asia, Oceania, and Central America, she lived in Darwin, Australia, before finally settling in the Netherlands.

Jennifer's love of travel, art, and culture inspires her award-winning Zelda Richardson Mystery series, her Travel Can Be Murder Cozy Mysteries, and her standalone stories. Her background in journalism, multimedia development, and art history enriches her novels.

When not writing, she can be found in a museum, biking around Amsterdam, or enjoying a coffee along the canal while planning her next research trip.

For more information about the author and her upcoming novels, please visit Jennifer's website. [http://jennifersalderson.com]

Sign up for her mailing list [http://eepurl.com/cWmc29] to receive updates on future releases, as well as a FREE digital copy of *Holiday Gone Wrong*.

Books by Jennifer S. Alderson:

Travel Can Be Murder Cozy Mysteries
Death on the Danube: A New Year's Murder in Budapest
Death by Baguette: A Valentine's Day Murder in Paris
Death by Windmill: A Mother's Day Murder in Amsterdam
Death by Bagpipes: A Summer Murder in Edinburgh
Death by Fountain: A Christmas Murder in Rome

Death by Leprechaun: A Saint Patrick's Day Murder in Dublin
Death by Flamenco: An Easter Murder in Seville
Death by Gondola: A Springtime Murder in Venice
Death by Puffin: A Bachelorette Party Murder in Reykjavik

Zelda Richardson Art Mysteries
The Lover's Portrait: An Art Mystery
Rituals of the Dead: An Artifact Mystery
Marked for Revenge: An Art Heist Thriller
The Vermeer Deception: An Art Mystery

Adventures in Backpacking Travel Thrillers
Down and Out in Kathmandu: A Backpacker Mystery
Holiday Gone Wrong: A Short Travel Thriller
Notes of a Naive Traveler: Nepal and Thailand Travelogue

Death on the Danube: A New Year's Murder in Budapest

Book One of the Travel Can Be Murder Cozy Mystery Series

Who knew a New Year's trip to Budapest could be so deadly? The tour must go on—even with a killer in their midst...

Recent divorcee Lana Hansen needs a break. Her luck has run sour for going on a decade, ever since she got fired from her favorite job as an investigative reporter. When her fresh start in Seattle doesn't work out as planned, Lana ends up unemployed and penniless on Christmas Eve.

Dotty Thompson, her landlord and the owner of Wanderlust Tours, is also in a tight spot after one of her tour guides ends up in the hospital, leaving her a guide short on Christmas Day.

When Dotty offers her a job leading the tour group through Budapest, Hungary, Lana jumps at the chance. It's the perfect way to ring in the new year and pay her rent!

What starts off as the adventure of a lifetime quickly turns into a nightmare when Carl, her fellow tour guide, is found floating in the Danube River. Was it murder or accidental death? Suspects abound when Lana discovers almost everyone on the tour had a bone to pick with Carl.

But Dotty insists the tour must go on, so Lana finds herself trapped with nine murder suspects. When another guest turns up dead, Lana has to figure out who the killer is before she too ends up floating in the Danube...

Available as paperback, large print edition, eBook, and in Kindle Unlimited.

Excerpt from *Death on the Danube*
Chapter One: A Trip to Budapest

December 26—Seattle, Washington

"You want me to go where, Dotty? And do what?" Lana Hansen had trouble keeping the incredulity out of her voice. She was thrilled, as always, by her landlord's unwavering support and encouragement. But now Lana was beginning to wonder whether Dotty Thompson was becoming mentally unhinged.

"To escort a tour group in Budapest, Hungary. It'll be easy enough for a woman of your many talents."

Lana snorted with laughter. *Ha! What talents?* she thought. Her resume was indeed long: disgraced investigative journalist, injured magician's assistant, former kayaking guide, and now part-time yoga instructor—emphasis on "part-time."

"You'll get to celebrate New Year's while earning a paycheck and enjoying a free trip abroad, to boot. You've been moaning for months about wanting a fresh start. Well, this is as fresh as it gets!" Dotty exclaimed, causing her Christmas-bell earrings to jangle. She was wrapped up in a rainbow-colored bathrobe, a hairnet covering the curlers she set every morning. They were standing inside her living room, Lana still wearing her woolen navy jacket and rain boots. Behind Dotty's ample frame, Lana could see the many decorations and streamers she'd helped to hang up for the Christmas bash last night. Lana was certain that if Dotty's dogs hadn't woken her up, her landlord would have slept the day away.

"Working as one of your tour guides wasn't exactly what I had in mind, Dotty."

"I wouldn't ask you if I had any other choice." Dotty's tone switched from flippant to pleading. "Yesterday one of the guides and two guests crashed into each other while skibobbing outside of Prague, and all are hospitalized. Thank goodness none are in critical condition. But the rest of the group is leaving for Budapest in the morning, and Carl can't do it on his own. He's just not client-friendly enough to pull it off. And I need those five-star reviews, Lana."

Dotty was not only a property manager, she was also the owner of several successful small businesses. Lana knew Wanderlust Tours was Dotty's favorite and that she would do anything to ensure its continued success. Lana also knew that the tour company was suffering from the increased competition from online booking sites and was having trouble building its audience and generating traffic to its social media accounts. But asking Lana to fill in as a guide seemed desperate, even for Dotty, and even if it was the day after Christmas. Lana shook her head slowly. "I don't know. I'm not qualified to—"

Dotty grabbed one of Lana's hands and squeezed. "Qualified, shmalified. I didn't have any tour guide credentials when I started this company fifteen years ago, and that hasn't made a bit of difference. You enjoy leading those kayaking tours, right? This is the same thing, but for a while longer."

The older lady glanced down at the plastic cards in her other hand, shaking her head. "Besides, you know I love you like a daughter, but I can't accept these gift cards in lieu of rent. If you do this for me, you don't have to pay me back for the past two months' rent. I am offering you the chance of a lifetime. What have you got to lose?"

* * *

The Lover's Portrait: An Art Mystery

Book One in the Zelda Richardson Art Mystery Series

"*The Lover's Portrait* is a well-written mystery with engaging characters and a lot of heart. The perfect novel for those who love art and mysteries!" – Reader's Favorite, 5-star medal

"Well worth reading for what the main character discovers—not just about the portrait mentioned in the title, but also the sobering dangers of Amsterdam during World War II." – IndieReader

A portrait holds the key to recovering a cache of looted artwork, secreted away during World War II, in this captivating historical art thriller set in the 1940s and present-day Amsterdam.

When a Dutch art dealer hides the stock from his gallery – rather than turn it over to his Nazi blackmailer – he pays with his life, leaving a treasure trove of modern masterpieces buried somewhere in Amsterdam, presumably lost forever. That is, until American art history student Zelda Richardson sticks her nose in.

After studying for a year in the Netherlands, Zelda scores an internship at the prestigious Amsterdam Historical Museum, where she works on an exhibition of paintings and sculptures once stolen by the Nazis, lying unclaimed in Dutch museum depots almost seventy years later. When two women claim the same painting, the portrait of a young girl entitled *Irises*, Zelda is tasked with investigating the painting's history and soon finds evidence that one of the two women must be lying about her past. Before she can figure out which one it is and why, Zelda learns about the Dutch art dealer's concealed collection. And that *Irises* is the key to finding it all.

Her discoveries make her a target of someone willing to steal – and even kill – to find the missing paintings. As the list of suspects grows, Zelda realizes she has to track down the lost collection and unmask a killer if she wants to survive.

Available as paperback, audiobook, and eBook.

Excerpt from *The Lover's Portrait*
Chapter 1: Two More Crates

June 26, 1942

Just two more crates, then our work is finally done, Arjan reminded himself as he bent down to grasp the thick twine handles, his back muscles already yelping in protest. Drops of sweat were burning his eyes, blurring his vision. "You can do this," he said softly, heaving the heavy oak box upwards with an audible grunt.

Philip nodded once, then did the same. Together they lugged their loads across the moonlit room, down the metal stairs, and into the cool subterranean space below. After hoisting the last two crates onto a stack close to the ladder, Arjan smiled in satisfaction, slapping Philip on the back as he regarded their work. One hundred and fifty-two crates holding his most treasured objects, and those of so many of his friends, were finally safe. Relief briefly overcame the panic and dread he'd been feeling for longer than he could remember. Preparing the space and artwork had taken more time than he'd hoped it would, but they'd done it. Now he could leave Amsterdam knowing he'd stayed true to his word. Arjan glanced over at Philip, glad he'd trusted him. He stretched out a hand towards the older man. "They fit perfectly."

Philip answered with a hasty handshake and a tight smile before nodding towards the ladder. "Shall we?"

He is right, Arjan thought, *there is still so much to do.* They climbed back up into the small shed and closed the heavy metal lid, careful to cushion its fall. They didn't want to give the neighbors an excuse to call the Gestapo. Not when they were so close to being finished.

Philip picked up a shovel and scooped sand onto the floor, letting Arjan rake it out evenly before adding more. When the sand was an inch deep, they shifted the first layer of heavy cement tiles into place, careful to fit them snug up against each other.

As they heaved and pushed, Arjan allowed himself to think about the future for the first time in weeks. Hiding the artwork was only the first step; he still had a long way to go before he could stop looking over his shoulder. First, back to his place to collect their suitcases. Then, a short walk to Central Station where second-class train tickets to Venlo were waiting. Finally, a taxi ride to the Belgian border where his contact would provide him with falsified travel documents and a chauffeur-driven Mercedes-Benz. The five Rembrandt etchings in his suitcase would guarantee safe passage to Switzerland. From Geneva he should be able to make his way through the demilitarized zone to Lyon, then down to Marseilles. All he had to do was keep a few steps ahead of Oswald Drechsler.

Just thinking about the hawk-nosed Nazi made him work faster. So far he'd been able to clear out his house and storage spaces without Drechsler noticing. Their last load, the canvases stowed in his gallery, was the riskiest, but he'd had no choice. His friends trusted him—no, counted on him—to keep their treasures safe. He couldn't let them down now. Not after all he'd done wrong.

* * *